Martin's
Last
Chance

Martin's Last Chance

Heidi Schmidt

CHRISTIAN FOCUS PUBLICATIONS

Originally publisehd by BLB Verlag, Bibellesbund
Verlag Marienheide/Winterthur as Mircos letzte
Chance 1996

© 1999
ISBN 1-85792-425-8

Published by Christian Focus Publications Ltd,
Geanies House, Fearn, Tain, Ross-shire
IV20 1TW, Scotland, Great Britain

Cover design by
Cover illustration by T Fennell

Translated by Derry Brebner

Printed and bound in Great Britain
by Caledonian, Glasgow

Contents

A Rough Day

Rebekka was in a vile mood. She sat playing Solitaire, the only game that she could half master on her computer, and tried to get over her frustration. Strictly speaking, it wasn't actually her computer. It belonged to her brother, Daniel, but he was away on a class trip in another part of Germany and wouldn't even know that she'd been using it.

She sat fuming. It felt as bad as if someone had just told her that the corner shop would never stock her favourite Jelly Bears ever again. That would have seemed like the end of the world to her. Today, everything had gone badly wrong. It had begun with her oversleeping and being late for school that morning. Actually, she wouldn't have minded if she'd missed the whole biology lesson, but unfortunately it had only been late enough for her name to be noted in the class register.

'I suppose you spent too long observing plants growing in their natural habitat on your way to school, so you'd be better prepared for my lesson, child?' Herr Mertens, her biology teacher smirked. He had enjoyed that.

'Ha, ha - very funny!' Rebekka hated him. He

always treated her like a little kid. She wanted to strangle him whenever he called her "child" Oh well, it didn't really matter. She had only had her name noted and she couldn't help it if school always began so early.

In the third period they'd been given back the results of the Maths test: A five. Bother! She definitely wasn't going to let Mum find out. Luckily, she hadn't told her that she had a Maths test or she would have had to swot up all Monday afternoon and miss seeing a film. When you're fourteen, fourteen and three-quarters to be exact, your mother doesn't need to know everything. After all, Rebekka was supposed to be mature and independent by now.

But the final blow had come at lunchtime when Mum had announced that Gran was coming over. That was the absolute end for Rebekka. It was okay for other people to love their Grans to bits, but they didn't have hers! Rebekka wasn't fond of her, in fact she couldn't stand her! It was, after all, Gran's fault that she had been given such a stupid name. How many other kids were called Rebekka? She certainly didn't know any. But Gran, who was too religious anyway, had decided that they should give her a name from the Bible.

Rebekka was relieved that she had not been called something worse - 'Milcah' for instance- she'd heard that name once and could just imagine the boys in her class winding her up about that! Unfortunately, Mum had been sort of religious then and she'd thought that Gran's suggestion was fantastic. Well, now she had to live with this name day in, day out, and people could tease her about it to their hearts' content.

'Your parents must have called you 'Re Becker'

because they didn't get a little Boris Becker!' Boris Becker wouldn't have been famous when she was born, but nobody bothered about that fact.

The latest catchphrase was

'Rebekka, Rebekka,

She's always getting fatter!'

It was true that it didn't even rhyme properly, but it drove Rebekka mad.

Apart from that, one of Gran's worst faults was her religious rabbeting-on, and that really got up Rebekka's nose. If things were going well for Gran, she was "so thankful to God". If they weren't so good, she'd say, "God will carry me through. He knows what He is doing." Whenever she got word that Rebekka had an important exam at school, she would promise: "I'll pray for you. God will help you. You should trust Him!" It was always "God, God, God" all the time. Apparently Gran couldn't do a thing without him. That could really get on your nerves, even though you knew it was all rubbish anyway.

So Gran was to descend on them again. Rebekka had tried hard to escape before her arrival.

'I have to go over to Ina's to swot up History - we've got a test next week.'

But the attempt had backfired. Mum had somehow stupidly known that Ina had a music lesson and then an appointment at the orthodontist's that afternoon.

'Besides,' her Mum had said, 'Your Gran doesn't come very often. You can at least give her a couple of hours of your time, surely?'

Two hours with this religious maniac. No way! What a waste of a day! Rebekka looked at her watch. Ten to three. Knowing her Gran, she would arrive at any minute.

'Oh well, let's get on with it.' Rebekka sighed and switched off the computer just as the doorbell rang. It was too late to get out of it now - why was everything going wrong today?

'Well, little Becky, how are you?' Gran gave her a huge hug as Becky opened the door.

'Okay,' Rebekka said rather grumpily.

'Have you got problems at school?' was her next question. She had already detected the frustrated tone of voice.

'No, everything's fine.'

That was all she needed - having to tell Gran about the five in Maths! What she did in school was her own business. Gran should do her a favour and keep her nose out.

In the sitting room, Mum was putting out mouthwatering cakes, a peace offering to Rebekka for giving up her precious afternoon.. It was then that Gran started up.

'Oh Irene, you won't believe what a lovely church service we had last Sunday!'

Rebekka wanted to disappear up to her room right there and then. Gran had hardly arrived and already she was beginning her religious stuff. It was so annoying.

'You know,' the old lady continued undeterred, 'the young people took the service. They were all about your age, my little Becky pet. Maybe some were a little older.'

'They must be off their heads - taking a church service! They might as well join a monastery and be done with it!' Rebekka thought. But she only grunted, 'I'm sure it was very nice for you.'

'Wouldn't you like to come along some time?' Gran beamed. 'They have a weekly meeting where they play games, sing songs, read the Bible and things like that.'

'You've got to be joking! Playing babyish games and singing daft songs. Not on your life!' thought Rebekka.

'Gran,' she said, 'I've always got loads to do. I've got so much homework that I don't have any time for things like that!'

It was certainly the biggest whopper of a lie she'd told in at least two months and her Mum gave her a look to let her know exactly what she thought.

'The youth fellowship is always on in the evening. You're bound to have time then,' she commented, and Gran nodded enthusiastically.

'Why does she have to drop me in it? ' Rebekka thought. But of course Mum always took Gran's side.

'I'll think about it.' She wanted to bring the stupid topic to an end.

Gran beamed and felt that she had fulfilled her missionary duty for the day. But Mum hadn't finished.

'What did the young people actually do in the church service?' She wanted to know. Gran was immediately back in her element.

'They sang songs, played guitars and drums - a bit too loud maybe but it was lovely nevertheless!'

Drums in church! Rebekka couldn't help grinning at the thought. At least these guys seemed to know a thing or two about music!

'And then they showed slides of sheep. The theme was the Good Shepherd, you see,' Gran said, looking very enthusiastic.

'Strange,' thought Rebekka, 'did God have something

to do with agriculture? I always thought they only talked about God and things like that in church.'

Mum didn't seem to find anything peculiar about it at all. But Rebekka wasn't interested in this religious stuff. Her brother Daniel was a nicer person than she was - that kind of thing would suit him.

Daniel made an effort at school - how could anyone be bothered to do that! He was always nice and polite, never told lies when he was embarrassed, and he wouldn't dream of pinching a bag of Jelly Bears from old Frau Schilling's shop. He was really straight - but she had to admit that he could be a good friend and a real laugh, when Mum was getting on at her for something. He was often the one who understood her best when the rest of the family had it in for her.

Gran and Mum had meanwhile found another topic to discuss: - politics. Not exactly riveting, but an improvement on church services. Rebekka kept looking at her watch. Why did the time pass so excruciatingly slowly when Gran was here? Could old people influence the speed of time? You'd almost think it was true sometimes.

Rebekka was lost in her thoughts, thinking about the next day. Herr Jürgens, her class teacher, who was okay really, had announced that a new pupil would be joining them. Apparently, he had a heart condition. Why would a boy who'd got some kind of heart disease bother to attend school? Surely it would be best to stay in hospital if you were ill. Rebekka was curious to know what this guy would be like. Perhaps he would go around groaning in pain all the time. Well, she'd just have to wait and see.

It was a relief when Gran eventually went away. Now Rebekka really needed to relax, which meant putting on her music full blast, drinking ten glasses of cola, eating crisps, and browsing through her new *Bravo* magazine.

Rebekka didn't have the energy to do her homework. She'd copy it quickly tomorrow from one of her friends, Maren or Ina, before school. Or else she'd say that for some inexplicable reason she'd totally forgotten about it. School wasn't everything in life, after all. She grabbed a bag of Jelly Bears from her supply - she always had about five bags handy in case of emergencies, and was glad that this horrible day was almost over.

'Shouldn't you be doing your homework, Becky?' Her Mum shouted into her room. She had to shout because the music was so loud.

'I did it ages ago!' Rebekka shouted back. At least she could make the most of the evening.

THE BLUE BOY

Rebekka's alarm clock didn't ring very loudly and she nearly overslept again. She thought that she was just dreaming, and turned over and went back to sleep. But Mum, who slept incredibly lightly, heard the alarm clock sounding. When she went into Rebekka's room a good bit later to confirm her suspicions, she had to give her daughter a rude awakening.

'You'd better get a move on, my girl!' She urged Rebekka.

It really was high time to get up, particularly if you wanted to copy umpteen bits of homework from friends before school started. There was no time for cleaning her teeth or washing today. It was pointless anyway, because she always had something to eat when she got to school, and her hands usually got covered in ink. At record-breaking speed, she devoured a cheese, sausage and chocolate spread sandwich - she'd always liked a weird combination of food - and then she rushed off.

Maren was not exactly delighted to hand over her carefully done homework, but it was amazing what someone would do for a bag of liquorice. Rebekka had pinched it the day before yesterday from the corner shop.

'I'm curious to see this new fella. He's supposed to have heart trouble. If you give him a fright, he'll probably fall down dead!' Maren speculated.

'I don't think that's true, otherwise they would never send him to school. But maybe we'll always have to carry his bag for him because he's too weak to do it himself!'

'Well, I'm certainly not carrying his bag for him,' Rebekka said in a determined voice, 'I'm nobody's slave! My own is enough! You'd better hurry up - here's Jürgens coming!'

However, it wasn't Herr Jürgens who appeared a few seconds later but the biology teacher who was carrying a school bag. Walking beside him was a blonde boy.

'What's Mertens doing here?' Rebekka wondered. 'We've got Physics now!'

What a great start to the day! It would have to be this idiot of a biology teacher who was standing in for theirs, who was ill. She sighed. What a waste of time it had been quickly copying out all of the physics homework!

After the general commotion had died down, everyone stared at the new boy. Somehow he looked a bit peculiar. He had bluish lips and his face looked sort of pasty. Herr Mertens introduced him.

'This is Martin Baumann. He has moved here from the Bremen area and hopefully, he'll soon feel at home. I'm sure Martin will tell you anything else you want to know later on. Now, let's see where you can sit. Oh yes, there's a place free over there.' He indicated the chair beside Rebekka.

Rebekka was not exactly delighted at this, and when

Martin sat down, she couldn't help moving a little away from him. He really did look odd.

'Hi,' Martin said.

'Hi,' Rebekka mumbled back.

The biology lesson was boring as usual and Rebekka wasn't really concentrating. Every now and again she would sneak a look at Martin and wonder why he had such blue looking lips. When he glanced back at her, she quickly looked away again. She didn't want him to think that she was interested in him in any way.

'Can you name the different parts of the flower, child?'

Rebekka came back to earth with a jolt. Herr Mertens was standing in front of her, grinning, something he always did when he caught her not paying attention. Of course Rebekka couldn't remember what the botanical names were.

'Were you not listening, child?'

'Oh yes, I was, Papa!' She blurted out cheekily, and the class began to giggle.

Herr Mertens screwed up his face: 'Don't be impudent, child!'

'I'm not your child - fortunately,' Rebekka said. Herr Mertens blushed a little, and went silently back to his desk.

'Perhaps he's finally got the message,' she thought.

However, Herr Mertens was unbearable for the rest of the lesson.

'Can't he take a joke?' Martin whispered to Rebekka.

'No, the hereditary factor for humour is probably missing in his DNA!'

Even Rebekka knew what that was because she'd seen the film 'Jurassic Park'. Martin grinned at her.

Perhaps he was okay after all.

For the next lesson the class had to traipse over to the large music room in the primary school building, mainly because Herr Deetz thought he could keep a better eye on them there. He could also occasionally play some pieces of music for them on the piano there.

Rebekka reluctantly slung her rucksack on to her back and strolled off. A music lesson was just what she needed to send her to sleep. She could never remember what sharps and flats were anyway, let alone how chords were formed. She tossed her bag down into the first space she could find outside the music room. At least they had a five minute break now. Then she caught sight of Martin, who had just arrived. He was leaning against the nearest radiator, totally out of breath. Rebekka was shocked. Martin was gasping, as if he'd just run a 1000 metres race, and his face had turned really blue.

'Gosh, you've turned blue. Are you ill?' she asked.

'I'll be alright in a minute,' wheezed Martin, 'I'm always like this if I've exerted myself.'

'But we haven't done anything strenuous. We've only walked over here. It wasn't exactly a 400 metres race!'

'But for me that's quite a lot. Well, it doesn't really matter. What's your name by the way?'

'I'm not telling you - I've got a really stupid one!'

'Oh come on, tell me!'

'Okay, but don't you dare laugh and make fun of it!'

'Okay, I promise!'

'My name's Rebekka but you can just call me Bekki.'

'I don't know what you're bothered about. Rebekka's a lovely name.'

'I think it's dumb. Everyone winds me up about it.'

'But it suits you,' Martin smiled. 'The name Rebekka is mentioned in the Bible and she was a beautiful girl.'

Rebekka felt herself going bright red. How embarrassing! This always happened whenever anybody said something nice - her face would suddenly turn the colour of an overripe tomato.

'How do you know that it's a biblical name? Do you read the Bible?' She quickly changed the subject.

'Yes,' Martin said, as casually as if she'd just offered him a bit of chocolate. Rebekka found this hard to believe.

'So you believe in God, Jesus and all that stuff, then?'

'Yes, God is like a father to me and Jesus is my best friend. I can tell him everything and he looks after me.'

Rebekka stared at him as if he was an alien who had just stepped out of a UFO. Up until now she'd thought that Martin was a relatively normal person. 'Believing in God at his age,' she thought. Perhaps he belonged to some kind of sect.

'Do you have to collect money for some kind of master or go around selling magazines and stuff like that?'

Martin laughed. 'No, I'm just a Christian.'

'So what does that mean?'

'Well, I talk to God about everything - things that I'm happy or sad about. Sometimes I ask him what he thinks about certain things. The same kind of things that you probably talk about with your best friend.'

'But you can't see or hear God, can you?'

'I don't need to be able to see him. It sounds silly, but I just know that he exists. And what you said about not hearing him is true to an extent. I can't listen to him by using my ears but sometimes God speaks to me through other people, or else when I'm reading the Bible. I suddenly realise what God wants me to do. Em - that probably sounds very strange to you, doesn't it? I can't explain it very well - you would really have to experience it for yourself.'

'Strange,' Rebekka thought. The most she'd ever had to do with praying was a grace occasionally said before meals, or reciting the Lord's Prayer. It was difficult to imagine herself speaking to God when she couldn't even see him. But then, her Gran was inclined to do that sort of thing. Martin did seem a bit weird, but somehow she quite liked him.

The bell went at this point and they saw Herr Deetz tearing around the corner. He was one of the few teachers who always arrived on time, a fact which he seemed to take a pride in.

After everybody was seated in the music room, Herr Deetz welcomed the new boy, and then started droning on as usual. Rebekka found it hard to concentrate. Anyway she couldn't care less about minor chords. Every now and then she sneaked a look at Martin. When he smiled back at her, she immediately focused her eyes on the front of the room again, and tried to look as if she found the topic incredibly interesting. His skin colour was back to normal again.

'I wonder if he asks God how to form chords?' She thought and grinned to herself. But why not really, if he was in the habit of discussing everything with his God.

Martin had somehow spoken so naturally about his relationship with God. He didn't seem to have the slightest doubt that he really existed. It was the first time that anyone had spoken to her about personal beliefs in such a laid back way. Her Gran always made stuff about God sound so above her head - as if only very saintly people could have anything to do with it - Martin made it sound much more straightforward. But she didn't want to think about it any more. Thankfully, this lesson would be finished in ten minutes and then it was break time.

It was fairly cold, but the teachers who were supervising them showed no mercy and ruthlessly sent the pupils outside for fresh air. Once outside, Rebekka looked round to see where Martin was. She wanted to continue her conversation with him - it was interesting somehow. She spotted him, huddled against the wall in a corner of the playground, looking freezing cold. When she got nearer to him she noticed his face and hands.

'You've turned blue again! We haven't done anything to tire you out, unless you've jogged once around the playground, have you?'

'No, I can't stand the cold. It always makes me feel shattered.'

'You should go inside, then. I'm sure they'll make an exception to the rule when they see you!'

'Leave it out - I don't want any special favours. I'll be okay - what subject do we have next'

'Geography - it's about as exciting as an eight hour bus trip with deaf pensioners!'

Martin grinned. 'You don't like school very much , do you?'

'Well, school is like a circus - only clowns go there!'

'What are you doing in Geography right now?'

'Something about tropics and subtropics - stuff like that. I'm not the best person to ask.'

Several boys from Rebekka's class suddenly appeared. Kai, the tallest of them, looked Martin up and down and then remarked: 'What have we got here then? You look revolting - blue hands and mouth - disgusting! Are you a Martian or something?'

'No,' said Martin 'I'm just such a dedicated Hamburg United football fan that even my skin is blue and white!' Martin then turned and walked away quietly.

Kai stood there looking sheepish.

'He's quick off the mark, I'll give him that,' commented Stefan, who was standing beside him.

'You're a right idiot!' Rebekka yelled into Kai's face and then stalked off to the classroom. Break time would be over in a minute or so anyway.

MARTIN

Rebekka was sitting at her desk doing homework. English was the only subject that she quite enjoyed, probably because she had fallen in love with her teacher. This guy was gorgeous to look at: about 1.80 metres tall, blonde, with wavy hair, bright blue eyes and a body like Arnold Schwarzenegger's, well almost. The only drawback, unfortunately, was that he happened to be married. 'Hardly surprising - the best ones are always snapped up first,' Rebekka thought. The chances of him getting divorced because of her were probably extremely slim. In spite of that, she really made an effort at English, just in case.

But today Rebekka's mind was elsewhere. She kept finding herself thinking about Martin. At lunch time she'd wanted to ask Mum why he looked so blue, but as usual, her mother had been too busy to talk about it. Mum never had time anyway. She always had something hugely important to do, just when Rebekka wanted to speak to her. Funny how she was very interested if it was about her school grades. She took an interest in these because she wanted her daughter to make something of herself.

Rebekka's parents were wealthy and respectable, and this 'family reputation', as she called it, was something that she'd found extremely irritating. It was also the reason why she didn't bother to make an effort these days.

So she sat and thought about Martin. He was a strange guy really - the slightest thing would make him turn blue and gasp for breath, so much, that you almost held your breath yourself. If God was really his best friend, wouldn't he make sure that Martin was healthy? Martin didn't seem to question this himself. He took everything very calmly as if it was the most natural thing in the world. She would have to ask him why he didn't complain to God about his life being so miserable.

'Bekki, can you do a bit of shopping for me?' She heard her Mum shouting from the kitchen.

'Can't you go yourself? I'm doing my homework at the moment,' Rebekka called back.

'I can't. I'm in the middle of baking a cake and my hands are sticky. And I've just realised that I've run out of cream and sugar. Come on, run and get them for me. My purse is lying in the hall cupboard. Please hurry up!'

It was typical of her Mother to be so scatterbrained, starting to bake a cake, before she'd even made sure that she had all the ingredients. What a hassle! Rebekka quickly pulled on her jacket, took the purse and tore off.

It took only three minutes to get to the shop. When she got there, she picked up the things she needed, furtively shoved a bag of Jelly Bears into her pocket and then went to the check-out. Then she saw Martin standing a little in front of her.

'Hi, Martin, what are you doing here?' She yelled so

loudly that everyone turned round and stared at her. Rebekka turned bright red again. How embarrassing!

Martin turned round too and said, 'Hi, Rebekka - shopping as well?'

When they were outside, Rebekka asked, 'Do you live near here?'

'Yes, just round the corner in the detached red house.'

'Really? Then we're more or less neighbours! I didn't realise that you'd moved in there. Here, would you like some Jelly Bears?' She pulled the bag out of her pocket.

'Thanks. I didn't notice you buying these.'

'I didn't. I pinched them. The idiots in there never notice,' Rebekka laughed.

But instead of laughing, Martin suddenly looked serious and said, 'In that case, I don't want any! I don't like stuff that has been nicked!'

'You call that stealing! It doesn't hurt anyone. They've got so many of them - they'll never even notice!'

'It's still stealing. Think about it. Everything that you steal is added onto the cost of the products. So others have to pay more. Which means you're to blame for it.'

Rebekka didn't like Martin's attitude. 'I didn't think you were such a goody-goody! You're worse than my brother. At least he eats what I pinch. Do you have to be like that because your God tells you to?'

'Well, maybe. God obviously doesn't want me to steal. But I don't like that kind of thing myself, either.'

'Forget it then.' Rebekka shoved the Jelly Bears back into her pocket. At least she could eat the things later herself.

'But I wanted to talk to you anyway - about your God and things like that.'

At this point it suddenly occurred to her that her Mum needed the cream and sugar urgently, so she shouted as she ran off, 'Can I maybe come round later? About five?'

'Sure. See you then,' Martin shouted, as she disappeared.

'You've come back at last! I've been waiting ages for you! Give me the things - quickly!' Rebekka's mother stood impatiently in the kitchen, splattered with cake-mix, flour, milk and cherry juice. Her baking always tasted fantastic, but her clothes ended up looking as if they'd been specially designed for a washing-powder test.

Rebekka sat down at her desk again. She put the bag of Jelly Bears down beside her English book. But amazingly, she'd lost her appetite, an extremely rare occurrence. 'Goody-goody!' She muttered under her breath. She soon finished her English homework and then turned to the German essay - "The Rights of the Powerful."

'Only Frau Schumann could think up such a ridiculous topic,' she groaned. The problem was that she couldn't copy Maren's essay. Frau Schumann had an unfortunate habit of gathering in their jotters and would notice straight away if she did.

Rebekka had no overwhelming desire to do her head in thinking about the rights of the powerful. Besides it was nearly five, and she'd be going round to Martin's soon. So she only wrote two sentences: 'Because I'm usually the weaker one, I've no idea about the rights of the powerful. You should ask my big brother instead!' There, that was it finished. It was Schumann's own fault for setting such stupid topics to write about. Oh yes, she had Maths homework to do as well. The only problem was how . Unfortunately, Maren was no brainbox when it came to Maths and neither was Ina. If she copied things from them, they were usually wrong. It was a silly situation really.

Then Rebekka had an idea. Perhaps Martin was good at Maths and she could copy the homework from him. Having made this quick decision, she packed her Maths books into a bag and marched off.

Feeling a bit unsure of herself, she pressed the Baumanns' doorbell. It was not really her style to make friends so quickly. A woman opened the door and smiled warmly at her. Rebekka liked her straight away.

'Hello, you've come to see Martin, haven't you? He told me that someone from his class was calling today. Come in.' Frau Baumann led the way to Martin's room.

'Martin, you've got a visitor. Do you want me to bring you something to drink?'

'Oh, nothing for me, thanks,' Rebekka declined, a little embarrassed. When Frau Baumann had left them, she added, 'Man - what room service you've got! I wish my mother was like that! Yours is okay!'

'I think so too,' Martin replied, smiling.

'Are you good at Maths?' Rebekka blurted out.

'Well, not bad. Why?'

'Can I copy the homework from you?'

'You can if you want to. I can explain it to you, if you like. It's not too difficult. You'll get more out of it that way.'

'Em - copying it would be faster.'

'But then you won't know how to do the next piece of homework. It's really pretty straightforward.'

'Okay, you've convinced me,' Rebekka admitted

defeat. Soon they were absorbed in the Maths. Rebekka had never dreamed that the subject could be fun. Once Martin had explained it to her, she found that it wasn't as difficult as she'd imagined.

When they had finished the homework, Rebekka looked around the room properly for the first time. She caught sight of a peculiar looking machine standing beside the bed.

'That's a weird looking vacuum cleaner.'

Martin laughed. 'It's not a vacuum cleaner - it's my oxygen machine.'

'Your what?'

'My oxygen machine. I get extra oxygen from it at night because my blood doesn't have enough in it.'

'How does it work?'

'Wait - I'll show you.' Martin put on a mask which was connected by a tube to the machine, and switched the machine on. It immediately began to make a whirring sound.

'What a grating noise! And you're supposed to be able to sleep with that going on?'

'You get used to it. But to be honest, I feel it doesn't really help me. I was actually okay without the thing. But perhaps it's helping me somehow, and it doesn't bother me now that it's on when I'm sleeping.'

Rebekka screwed up her face. She wouldn't want to have such a creepy looking box in her room.

'What kind of illness do you have exactly? Jürgens said you had heart trouble or something.'

'That's right,' Martin answered, switching off the machine and sitting at his desk. 'I have a hole in the heart, so the good blood which has enough oxygen in it

27

gets mixed in with the blood that has already been used which doesn't have so much oxygen in it. That's the reason why I usually look sort of blueish. The name of the disease is Atrial Septal Defect or ASD for short.'

'But can't they do anything about it? I mean, can't they operate or something?'

'They could have operated on me when I was a baby, but because I was so weak, I would never have survived the operation. The doctors told my parents that they would be able to operate when I reached a certain weight.'

'And why didn't you have the operation?'

'When I eventually weighed enough, my parents were naturally over the moon about it. But then the doctors suddenly told them that it was too late for an operation because of a change of pressure in the blood vessels. Anyway, an operation's been out of the question since then because of the likelihood of complications'

'Your parents must have been very upset when they heard that.'

'Of course - they had a fright. Then I was ill for months on end and they were often afraid that I wouldn't survive another hour. I think that if they hadn't relied on God so much, and trusted that He was doing the right thing, they wouldn't have come through it so well. It was really hard for them.'

Rebekka stared at the floor, deeply affected by this. If she'd had a baby who was as seriously ill as that ...

'But you're surely a lot better now, compared with what you were like then.'

'Yes, I made a good recovery - it was like a miracle had happened. The doctors can't understand it to this day. I'm sure that God had a hand in it.'

Martin always had to bring his God into everything!

'If God is really your father like you claimed he was this morning, surely he would see to it that you were reasonably healthy. Instead, he's given you this horrible disease! I wouldn't want to have a father like that!' Rebekka was interested to see how Martin would react to that.

'Em . . . I admit that I don't always understand it, but then He wouldn't be God, if I could. But I trust that He wants the best for me in spite of everything. It says in the Bible that all things work together for good for those who love Him. You know, Bekki ...' Rebekka blushed a little. He'd called her Bekki for the first time! 'I've often experienced God's help because of my illness. He's also given me a lot of good things . . . My family, for example, friends, some brains and good ideas to keep me occupied and other things too. Some healthy people don't have these things. Because of my illness I'm a bit more dependent on God, and that's a good thing too. If that hadn't been the case, I might have lost my faith ages ago.'

'You've certainly got a fixation with God. You sound as if you couldn't live without Him.'

'I couldn't. But I wouldn't want to live without Him, because having God in your life is the best thing that can happen to you. You can take it from me, Bekki.'

'I don't know . . .' On one hand, Rebekka was impressed at how naturally Martin spoke about his faith, but on the other, she wasn't even sure if God existed. Perhaps some bloke had invented the whole story about God.

'How do you know that He really exists? You've

never seen Him, have you?'

'No, but I've experienced so much with God that I must simply believe he's there. For instance, the doctors always said that I wouldn't live long. At first, they thought I wouldn't even reach my first birthday. Then they said I would only live until I was five at most, then eight, then twelve. I'm fifteen now and I'm still alive. That's just one example. Often I encounter God in everyday things. Sometimes He does things that make me keel over in amazement! I know that I can totally rely on him. That helps me to view difficult situations in a different light and not to panic.'

Rebekka thought for a moment. 'Hm, I would quite like it if God did something for me. Perhaps I could believe in Him then.' Suddenly she caught sight of her watch. 'Good grief, it's almost half past six - we always have supper then. My mother is very keen on us being on time. I'd better get over there fast. See you tomorrow. Thanks for explaining the Maths!'

'You're welcome. It was nice to have you here. See you tomorrow!'

And Rebekka disappeared.

KAI CAUSES
MORE TROUBLE

Martin had been part of the class for two months, and by now everyone was used to the blue appearance of his skin. Only Kai kept on making snide remarks and trying to annoy him whenever possible. Sometimes he bombarded him with bits of paper, or empty cartons. He was probably just too lazy to put them in the litter bin. Occasionally he tried to trip up Martin as well. Apparently Kai had always been looking for someone to bully and now he had found someone.

'Weaklings like you should be put down! Morons like you are just a burden for everyone! You're scum! You look disgusting - get out of my sight!'

Sometimes a few of the other pupils began to retaliate by insulting Kai when he came out with such coarse expressions. 'Stop it, you idiot! You're really dumb!'

Martin never said a word, except on one occasion when he remarked, 'Honestly, Kai, I feel sorry for you because you're so stupid.'

Kai glared at him full of hatred and shouted into his

face, 'And I feel sorry for you because you're so ugly!'

'I'd rather be ugly than stupid,' Martin said calmly, and turned and went away.

'Why do you never really try to defend yourself?' Rebekka asked him.

'In the first place, Kai's a lot stronger than me, and secondly, there's no point in hitting back. To be honest with you, I really do feel sorry for the guy.'

'You're sorry for that fool?'

'Yes, because he's not happy himself.'

'How do you know that?' Rebekka asked in astonishment.

'Well, think about it. When someone's really happy, he doesn't cause trouble. People who are happy don't usually want others to have a hard time.'

'There's probably some truth in that but I'd try to get my own back on him, somehow.'

'That would only make things worse. It's probably better if I pray that God will bring happiness into Kai's life.'

'Martin, you've got to admit that you really talk rubbish, sometimes. But if you ever change your mind, you can count on me.'

'Thanks, Bekki.'

A good friendship had developed between Martin and Rebekka. She even put up with the fact that he nearly always brought God into everything. Sometimes she found herself wishing that she was able to face life as calmly as Martin did. For instance, the way Martin took all Kai's taunts without losing his head. If she had been in his shoes, she would have told Kai what she really thought of him ages ago. She and her friends would have beaten him up in some dark corner by now, or even something worse.

'Do you think, that it's for your good when Kai pesters you constantly like this?' She whispered to Martin during biology.

'Em - I suppose it must be, although I don't really understand how. The whole thing's slowly doing my head in. I'm happy on the days that I don't have to face him.'

Martin glanced over at Kai, who was in the process of scribbling something on a piece of paper. Judging by the nasty way he was sniggering, it obviously wasn't very complimentary.

'I sympathise with you, but you won't let us beat some sense into the guy.'

The bell went for break time. What a relief it was to hear that sound, especially after biology. Now they had to go over to their own classroom for English with the man of her dreams.

'Come on, I'll carry your bag for you - you look pretty shattered today.' Rebekka was just about to take Martin's bag when Kai snatched it from under her nose, and ran off in the direction of the classroom.

'Hey - you pig! Give me the bag back right now!' Rebekka bawled after him, but Kai had long since disappeared.

'Leave it. It doesn't matter - I'll get it later on,' Martin tried to calm her down.

'Yes, but it's just a matter of when and how!'

They walked slowly towards the classroom. When they turned the corner, they were confronted with a terrible mess: Kai had scattered the entire contents of the bag all over the corridor. He had also shunted Martin's desk and chair down to the far end of the corridor.

'Well, you cretin, you've made it here at last! Wheeze, wheeze!' sneered Kai, who was standing in the doorway.

That was the last straw for Rebekka. Screaming swear words at him, she seized him by the collar and shook and kicked him. He was much stronger than her and she was amazed that she'd had the guts to do it.

Kai was totally thunderstruck, and so taken aback that he didn't even try to defend himself. In the meantime, Martin had begun to pick up his belongings, and it wasn't long before several boys came to his rescue. Martin was especially thankful that the others carried his desk and chair back into the classroom - they would have been far too heavy for him.

By the time Rebekka's dream man walked into the classroom everything was back in its place, and even Martin had recovered from his exertions.

Kai sat silently at his desk and didn't look once at Rebekka or Martin during the whole lesson. Rebekka had already dismissed the whole incident from her mind, and was trying to make every effort to concentrate. Herr Mertens would have died of jealousy, if he'd seen her paying so much attention.

She wondered how she could get to know Herr Becker better. That was his name, although Rebekka thought that it was much too ordinary for a man like him. Besides, if he really did get a divorce and married her - Rebekka Becker - that would sound really stupid! Well, it was only a dream anyway. He didn't seem to take any particular notice of her, even though she really made an effort. What irritated her most were the times when he'd talk about his wife and three children, of whom he seemed very fond. It was too bad that all the good looking and nice men were either too old, or spoken for already, or both. When would she ever meet a man like him?

Martin sussed out very quickly that Rebekka was giving Herr Becker interested looks, and he started to grin.

'You're very interested in old Becker, aren't you?' He asked quietly.

Once again, Rebekka's face could have competed with the ripest tomato. Luckily, Herr Becker didn't seem to notice.

'He seems like a nice bloke,' Martin added quickly, and Rebekka smiled. Sometimes Martin got it right.

Unfortunately, the English period was over after forty-five minutes, just like any other lesson. But English always seemed to go past particularly quickly.

During break time Kai was very quiet, and not a single stupid comment passed his lips.

The bell rang for German. Not exactly Rebekka's favourite subject. But at least Frau Schumann was so scatterbrained that she never detected her pupil secretly writing letters under the desk, doodling, or copying out homework. Today, however, to Rebekka's great dismay, Frau Schumann came in carrying a heap of essay jotters. She'd completely forgotten that they had a test! Well, no letter writing today. Hopefully, they would get a decent topic this time. Perhaps it would be "The injustice that the weaker person suffers".

'Morning! Henning, get your feet off the desk! And Sandra, put away that half-eaten apple!'

After the usual pleasantries from their teacher they had to begin. The topic was "What is a genuine friend?"

That was a bit of luck because it was a fairly relevant topic. But how would you actually describe a real friend? Rebekka thought for a moment. Firstly, a friend had to be someone you could trust, and who you could rely on. And then of course he'd have to have the same interests - or at least some of them. And naturally he'd help if you had problems.

Rebekka thought about Martin and the incident with Kai. She'd helped him. He gave her a hand with Maths and Physics. Were they friends? She glanced at Martin and he smiled back. Yes, they really were friends. She realised that she could trust him. Only he didn't have the same interests. Instead of reading *Bravo* magazine, he read the Bible. That was one of the things that worried her the most - a normal, nice bloke reading a totally boring book and religious magazines, which she had to admit didn't look too bad. Instead of going to the disco, he preferred to go to the cinema or somewhere else with some of the young people from his church, and instead of playing tennis, he played panpipes.

Rebekka scored out the sentence in her jotter abut having the same interests. Perhaps that wasn't so important after all. What other factors made someone a real friend? She slipped Martin a note, on which she'd written 'What do *you* think a real friend is?' Shortly afterwards, she had the note returned to her with the answer written on it, 'For me the best kind of friend would be someone who loves me and would do anything for me, even though he knew every last detail about me.' Rebekka read the sentence over several times until she understood what it meant. She looked at Martin and brooded over what he'd written. If someone really knew her through and through - all the bad thoughts and things that nobody else knew about her, would they still be able to love her? After thinking for a while, she wrote Martin another note - 'Such a friend doesn't exist!'

Martin slipped the note back again, having added, 'Yes, there is - God!'

'I should have seen that coming,' Rebekka thought. Was God (if he existed) really such a good friend?

THE LAST CHANCE

'Who's away today?' Herr Jürgens was taking the class register as usual.

'Martin's got a hospital checkup,' Rebekka explained her friend's absence.

'I know, he told me yesterday.'

Recently Rebekka had been wishing more and more that something could be done to help Martin. When he sat there turning blue and gasping for breath, she felt really sorry for him. Today he was at yet another appointment at the university hospital. She wondered what they actually did to him there. She'd asked him the day before and he'd replied, 'Oh, just a blood test, an examination, electrocardiograms, X-rays and stuff like that. Nothing exciting. Most of the time you have to sit around waiting.'

Why couldn't they do anything to help him, even at a university clinic? And, Rebekka kept asking herself the question which troubled her even more, if this God in whom Martin so firmly believed really existed, why didn't he help him?

'If you are there, God,' she thought, 'then please let

the doctors discover something today that will help Martin!' Was that a prayer? Perhaps it was. If God existed, and if he knew everybody's thoughts as Martin maintained, he would actually know what she'd asked for. The only question was whether he would respond.

The lesson went right over her head, and Rebekka realised that she was feeling quite tense and excited. She felt as if she would burst from sheer suspense, something she hadn't experienced since last seeing a horror film. She could hardly wait to see Martin again and to ask him how the appointment had gone. In her mind it was already the afternoon, and it didn't matter if her mind wandered in history, which was next. Herr Krom always spoke for hours about the same subjects in any case, so she would daydream instead about running a race with Martin in PE (of course, at the moment he was signed off PE) and she imagined him winning, without getting out of breath! That would be great. The more she thought about it, the more she realised that she'd grown very fond of Martin, even if he was a religious nutcase.

Even Kai seemed to miss having a victim to bully because during break time he just sat in a chair looking bad-tempered, and then he came shuffling over to Rebekka.

'So, Bekki, are you lonely without your darling?'

'Stupid idiot!' She retorted and continued to read the latest edition of her favourite magazine. Letting herself get wound up by Kai was the last thing she was in the mood for. The photo love-story was a whole lot more interesting.

'Now, now, watch your temper! Are you worried your boyfriend won't come back? Perhaps they'll keep him there and he'll kick the bucket. He always looks like he's about to anyway!'

Kai loved provoking Rebekka and interestingly enough he always managed to hit his victims' most vulnerable spot.

'Shut up and get out of my sight!' Rebekka shouted. But Kai had no intention of doing that. With a sneer he continued, 'He'll definitely not last much longer. If I was in your shoes, I'd find myself a new boyfriend. Otherwise, you're going to end up as a lonely old maid!'

That was the last straw! Without further ado, Rebekka got hold of her geography atlas and clouted it with full force on to Kai's skull. He fell to the ground and shouted, 'Have you had enough? Do you want to kill me?'

'It's your own fault, for always talking such rubbish!' Rebekka justified herself. 'If you won't listen!'

Luckily, the geography teacher came in at that point, so Kai didn't have time to retaliate. He sat down at his desk looking furious and rubbing the back of his head. It was beneath his dignity to drag the teacher into things. He'd get even with that girl. Unfortunately he wouldn't get the chance today because this was the last period and he always had to rush to catch his bus. But tomorrow was another day.

Rebekka phoned the Baumanns' house immediately after lunch.

'Sven Baumann speaking,' Martin's older brother answered the phone.

He was very nice too, as Rebekka had discovered. She didn't know any other family that stuck together like they did.

'Hi, Sven - it's Bekki. Is Martin back yet?'

'No, sorry. He probably won't get home until the evening. These appointments always drag on for quite a long time. Shall I tell him to phone you when he gets back?'

'Yes please. Are they trying to do something different with him today?'

'As far as I know, it's only the usual kind of thing. Why are you asking?'

'Em, I just wondered. Well, bye.'

'Yes, see you sometime.'

Disappointed, Rebekka put down the receiver. She had really hoped that they would carry out new kinds of tests on Martin today, and that the doctors would suddenly discover a method of operating which could help him. Oh well, she couldn't do anything about it.

Which homework did she really have to do? Rebekka's motto was 'Never do more than is really necessary.' She could copy Maths from Martin tomorrow if she didn't see him today, she could copy geography from Maren, history from Ina, and she had managed to do the German homework at school. That was the matter of homework disposed of. But what could she occupy herself with now? She didn't want to leave the house in case she missed Martin's phone call. Perhaps something crucial would have happened that could improve his health.

Perhaps there was something interesting on the telly. She'd have a look. Rebekka sat on her bed and fiddled with the remote control. Dad had given her the TV for Christmas, probably to try and make up for the fact that he never had time for her. But there was nothing worth watching, only boring kids' programmes and sports reports at this time of day. If they'd had cable TV she could have watched a good film. Why did they have to live in this tiny dump of a town?. It was probably the last place in the world to get cable TV. Very frustrating.

Perhaps she could play a game on Daniel's computer. She looked into his room. Noone there - that was a stroke of luck. Daniel was bound to be over at his girlfriend's house. Ever since he'd met her, he'd hardly been home. Rebekka got the game of solitaire up on to the screen and tried her best to play. But somehow, today it didn't seem to work. No wonder, she was constantly thinking about Martin. Eventually, she switched off the computer. There was simply no point in playing today.

Then she had a brainwave - how about playing a few tricks over the phone? That would pass the time and it might be quite funny. But then Martin wouldn't be able to get through, so she couldn't do that. Eventually she sat down in front of the telly and watched about seventeen different kids' programmes, constantly flicking from channel to channel. She didn't actually enjoy hopping from one to the next, but she had to kill time somehow.

It was just after four. What could she do now? Maybe she could read something. She scanned the bookcase until she caught sight of an expensive looking book. It was the Bible which Gran had given her for her twelfth birthday. Who else would have given her a present like that? 'For your confirmation classes,' she'd said. To be honest, Rebekka would have much preferred a hundred Mark note.

She stared at the book for ages and then took it out and leafed through the pages. She read a sentence here and there. 'Abraham begat Isaac, Isaac begat Jacob. . .'

Funny stuff to write about. She wondered where she could read about this Jesus or Martin Luther, who they were always talking about in church. She had reached page 734 but still hadn't read anything about him. Perhaps this wasn't a proper Bible. Maybe you had to look at the index to find out where you could read something about Jesus. The index confused Rebekka even more. It was divided into the Old Testament and the New Testament. She remembered that they had learned about it in confirmation classes at some point.

Why hadn't they simply written a book called for instance - 'The Story of God, Jesus and His People' and been done with it? What was the point of it being divided into testaments and books? After all, the Bible wasn't a novel in serial form, otherwise the next instalment would have to appear some time. "The ultra-new Testament" or something like that. She noticed there were even letters in the Bible. Their postal services couldn't have had very good security in those times. Rebekka had always loved snooping into other people's mail, including the love letters which her brother received from his girlfriend.

She decided to take a peek at one of these Bible letters. But which one should she choose? The Letter of Paul to the Romans - that sounded good. She'd heard about the Romans in History. Maybe there would be accounts of gladiator fights and battles in it.

After a considerable time leafing through the pages, she eventually found the letter. But there was nothing about wars and contests in it. Even Julius Caesar, the chap in the *Asterix* comics didn't feature in it. Instead of that, Paul somebody was writing about Jesus - at least there was something written here about him. Feeling disappointed, Rebekka turned over a few pages. Some sentences were in bold print and she read a few of them. They seemed to be the ones that were particularly important. Suddenly, she came across a sentence which seemed very familiar to her: 'We know that all things work together for good to those who love God.' Wasn't that exactly what Martin always said?

The shrill tone of the telephone made her jump.

'Rebekka Jansen,' she answered.

'Hello, Bekki. It's Martin here. You called me?'

Rebekka suddenly became quite excited again. What if something new had been discovered?

'I just wanted to know if your doctors told you that there might be something new . . .?'

'I do have an amazing piece of news! Shall I tell you?'

What a question! Rebekka was so excited that she completely forgot to reply.

'Bekki, are you still there?'

'Of course,' she said at last, 'Please tell me what's happened!'

'Well,' Martin began, 'the doctors told me that I might have a chance if I go through a fairly major operation.'

'What kind of operation?' Rebekka wanted to know, after she'd shouted for joy inwardly.

Martin hesitated. 'Don't get excited, Bekki. It sounds quite bad. They think I need a heart and lung transplant. The heart and lungs of somebody who has perhaps been killed in an accident will have to be transplanted into me.'

Rebekka had to swallow hard, and she felt a bit dizzy.

'Does it have to be like that . . . I mean, are there no other possibilities?'

'No. They told me straight out that I have only two years to live. But, look, after a transplant operation I'll be healthy, more or less. Then we'll be able to run to school together without me turning blue!' Martin tried to cheer her up. He really seemed to be happy about this possibility. Rebekka couldn't understand it at all.

'Wouldn't it be great if I was well at last? ... Bekki, are you still there?'

Rebekka couldn't say a word. In her mind's eye, when she pictured the surgeons cutting open Martin's body, removing his heart and lungs, and replacing them with somebody else's organs (some dead person!) She felt sick. The big question was whether he would survive all that.

'Martin,' she said eventually, 'are you sure that everything will go okay?'

'Bekki, you know . . . em . . . I'm sure God's in control of it all. It maybe sounds weird, but when the doctor suggested the transplant operation to me I felt incredibly happy about the prospect of being well. I don't actually know if this operation will go ahead either, because they need exactly the right organs. But if not . . .' Martin paused for a moment, and then calmly said, 'Then . . . Then I'll be with God and I'll be happy there. In any case, somehow I'm totally convinced that God will do the right thing.'

Rebekka felt like bursting into tears. She now became painfully aware of how attached to Martin she'd become.

'I don't want to lose you, Martin. You're a good friend!'

'I don't want to lose you either, Bekki! But a transplant operation is my only chance. And my last. I've no alternative. To be honest, I'm glad that something like this can be done for me. They never told me about it before. Bekki, just imagine the things we'll be able to do then! Try to look forward to that!'

Rebekka sniffed a little. 'If I only knew for sure that it would all be okay!'

'It'll definitely be okay. I have to go - it's supper time. We can talk about it tomorrow. See you, Bekki.'

'See you tomorrow, Martin,' Rebekka slowly hung up. She sat for ages and tried to take on board what she'd heard. Suddenly, she remembered what she'd prayed about that morning - for something to happen that would help Martin. Had God really listened to her prayer?

CAUGHT!

Rebekka was slowly getting used to the idea of the transplant operation. She couldn't allow herself to actually imagine it though.

'It must be a really weird feeling to have a different heart in your body. I would feel sick just thinking about it.'

It was strange to imagine that soon there might be a heart in Martin's chest, donated from someone who had died, pumping the blood around his body . . .

'Aren't you scared of this operation?'

'No, not really. I know it won't exactly be a party, but it won't last forever, and then hopefully I'll be better after it. Somehow, I'm completely sure that God is watching over every detail and that makes me feel sort of calm.'

Rebekka stared at him, feeling sceptical. He really did seem to have no fears.

'What will they do with you now? Will they ring you up and say, "Hi, Martin! Just pop over for the transplant operation now," or what will happen?'

'No, first of all they'll have to run masses of tests before I can get onto the waiting list. They have to check exactly what size the organs will need to be, and what kind of tissue suits me. And when they know all that important information, then hopefully I'll be put on the waiting list.'

'Are there a lot of people on it?'

'Yes, a lot more than there are organs available.'

That didn't sound very encouraging.

'And when you get onto the list, what happens then?'

'Then I'll just have to wait until they tell me that I can come for the transplant operation.'

Rebekka thought for a moment.

'Then you'll always have to stay at home - it'll be like being in prison.'

'No, I'm getting a pager. It'll be like the ones doctors have, a kind of emergency radiophone. They'll phone my house and my pager will bleep. I'll be able to take it with me everywhere.'

'That's a better idea. It would be really daft if you could only lounge around at home.'

Rebekka packed away her Maths homework which Martin had been helping her with.

'What shall we do now?' she asked.

'I've just remembered that I have to get a birthday present for my Mum. Do you want to go down to Merkers?'

Merkers was the large store where Rebekka "acquired" her Jelly Bears from time to time. You could buy just about anything there. In spite of this, everyone usually referred to the large store as "the shop". It was quite surprising that there was such a large store in a small country town.

'You can advise me. You've probably got more of an

idea what kind of things a woman likes.'

'Well, I like Jelly Bears and magazines, but I don't think they'd appeal to your Mother! I need to replenish my supplies of Jelly Bears anyway.'

Martin looked at her in disbelief and asked, sounding a little disappointed:

'Are you going to pinch them again?'

'Leave it out - that's my business!' Rebekka defended herself. 'I don't forbid you to read the Bible, do I?'

'I can't tell you not to do it. I just don't think it's right. Why do you do it? Don't you get any pocket money?'

'Of course, I do,' Rebekka admitted, 'I get 150 Marks a month. My folks are okay as far as pocket money is concerned.'

'What? 150 Marks? I only usually get 40 Marks. Man, I really don't understand you - why do you have to pinch things?'

'I only nick things for a laugh. It's their own fault for laying them out so that they can be taken easily. It's a cool feeling - you're itching to see if they're going to catch you or not. It's brilliant.'

'And what if they really did catch you?' Martin interrupted.

'Oh, rubbish! They'll never do that - they're too thick.'

Besides Rebekka knew she was clever enough not to get caught. She'd had years of practice after all. Martin took the 40 Marks which he'd saved up for his mother's birthday present and the two of them set off.

When they reached the shop, they went their separate ways. Rebekka hurried across to the Jelly Bears, while Martin looked round the household goods department. He was just wondering whether he should buy his mother heated rollers as that was the only thing which she didn't already have (although it was true that she didn't have curly hair), when he heard a man shouting: 'We've got you at last, little madam! So it's you who has been stealing stuff here! Well, I'm sure your parents will be delighted when they have to collect you from the police station!'

Martin turned round and caught sight of a man dragging Rebekka along by her jacket sleeve, and ran towards them straight away.

'What are you doing to my friend?'

The man stared at him scornfully.

'She's your girlfriend? Then I'd advise you to keep a closer eye on her the next time. We've just caught her stealing things - caught red-handed in fact. And it's certainly not the first time that she's stolen something!'

The man held up two bags of Jelly Bears and one bag of liquorice in front of Martin's face.

'How can you be sure that she intended to steal the bags of sweets? Perhaps she's got the habit of putting the bags in her pockets because she doesn't have a shopping trolley, and she meant to put them down on the counter when she came to the check-out.'

'Oh, so why doesn't she have any money with her then?'

Rebekka looked despairingly at Martin. Her prospects didn't look too good. And he'd even warned her today about this. If only she had listened to him!

'Because I'm paying for these things,' Martin said in a convincing tone of voice, and pulled out his wallet. He looked the man straight in the eyes. He wouldn't give in now!

'Well, okay' the man muttered. It was obvious that

this turn of events didn't please him at all. Reluctantly, he let go of Rebekka.

'But I'm warning both of you, you're for it the next time!'

He returned to his office without once glancing back at them.

Rebekka didn't know what to say. She felt completely ashamed, something that was usually totally alien to her. At the same time, she felt greatly relieved and grateful. When she imagined her father's reaction to finding out that she was a shoplifter (the company manager's daughter), she felt sick. That would have guaranteed a huge row and she would have been grounded for at least a month.

'Thanks,' she said quietly, eventually.

'It's okay, Bekki.'

Martin bought a box of chocolates and paid for everything at the check-out. Once they were outside again they walked along in silence for a while. Rebekka was surprised. She had expected a sermon or at least an 'I told you, but you wouldn't listen to me!' Or even a derisive look on Martin's face. But he said absolutely nothing.

'Why did you do that for me? It was all my own fault and you even warned me about it. Why did you come to my rescue anyway?' Rebekka asked him at last.

'I didn't want them to report you to the police,' Martin replied. 'You'd certainly have been in hot water then.'

'Martin, do you know something?'

'What?'

'You're a real friend! And do you know what else?'

'What?'

51

'I'll never pinch anything ever again. I hereby solemnly promise you.'

'Well, if you really manage to do that, I'm glad that I stood you the Jelly Bears,' Martin seemed to be genuinely pleased.

'Talking of Jelly Bears,' he grinned, 'I wouldn't mind one or two.'

Rebekka and Martin sat down in a nearby bus shelter so that they could eat the sweets in comfort. Rebekka already felt a whole lot better. When she really thought about it, shoplifting had been a stupid way of messing around, especially since it was something she hadn't really needed to do.

'Martin, I think you're really cool!' She beamed, and this time it was Martin who blushed for a change.

'I didn't realise that you could turn red as well!' Rebekka said mischievously.

'Have you never actually pinched something or lied yourself?' Rebekka asked after a while.

'Yes I have, quite often. But I've always regretted it afterwards,' Martin replied, and smiled to himself.

'When I was small, I used to play Cowboys and Indians with one of my friends. My friend had a fantastic penknife. I only had one carved out of a piece of wood. One day I just pinched the penknife from him.'

'From your friend? You're even worse than I am!' Rebekka interrupted, pretending to be outraged. She really hadn't believed him capable of doing something like that.

'And what happened then?' She wanted to know.

'I had a terribly guilty conscience, but I didn't have the courage to give the knife back to him. Then one day

I lost it, and I felt even more guilty then.'

Rebekka stared at him in astonishment. He'd felt guilty about a stupid little penknife? She really couldn't understand it. Well, it had been his friend's penknife, after all...

'What did you do then?'

'I couldn't face him any more. I even prayed that God wouldn't let me die, before I'd had enough courage to sort it all out.'

Rebekka had to laugh at how seriously he took everything. Martin laughed as well.

'The best part of the story is that when I eventually confessed to my friend what I'd done, he just said, "Oh, that old thing! I wanted to get rid of it anyway. I bought a much better one ages ago!"'

'You put yourself through all that for nothing then.'

'Yes, but in spite of that, it was a huge relief when everything was sorted out.'

Rebekka could relate to that, after what had happened to her in the shop that day.

'And when have you told lies?'

'I've lied quite often, even when I haven't really meant to. I'm inclined to exaggerate when I'm speaking about something. If there were 346 people somewhere, for instance, I'd probably say, "There were must have been almost 1,000 people there!"'

'Wow, that really is exaggerating!' Rebekka said, and winked. 'What does God actually do with you when you mess things up? Does he not speak to you any more?'

'No, he forgives me if I ask him to,' Martin replied.

'How? Just like that? But if someone does something wrong, then surely they deserve to be punished!' Even

Rebekka had a sense of justice.

'God has already punished someone else for it,' Martin explained.

'Really? That sounds a bit unfair. Who then?'

'Jesus!'

'Jesus?'

'Yes, you probably know that they crucified Jesus, don't you?'

'Of course!' Rebekka had learned that in one of the rare RE lessons they'd had. In the other lessons scheduled for RE, they'd had to lug chairs, clean up the playground and stuff like that.

'You see,' Martin continued, 'Jesus was punished for all the rotten things that people do. It was his own choice to die because he loved us so much. It was the only way possible for people to be able to come back to God again. God can't stand anything wrong near him.'

'I've never heard that before,' Rebekka stared intently down at her shoes. She always did that when she was thinking deeply about something. If Jesus had really died for other people, he must have really loved them. She wouldn't have done what he did, particularly as most people didn't even want to know anything about him. No one would find it easy to choose to die for others. It slowly began to dawn on her why Martin thought so highly of God and Jesus.

'Do you think Jesus loves me as much as he loves you, even though I've messed up a lot more than you have?'

'First of all, you've probably not done any more stupid things than I have - you don't really know me. You don't realise how mad I can get, and it's better for nobody to be near me when I'm like that. I'm certainly not one bit better than you. Secondly, I'm sure that Jesus loves you just as much as he loves me. He's just waiting for you to want to be his friend.'

Rebekka brooded over what he'd said. No, she didn't want to become a Christian. She would have to give up too much. Jesus probably didn't think much of horror films, copying homework, hard rock and lots of other cool things.

'I don't want to become a Christian yet - maybe later on - when I'm a bit older. I want to have a life.'

'Man, you're not asking for very much, are you! I don't just want 'a life' I want the best life possible! That's why I'm a Christian.'

What did he mean by that? Did Christians really get more out of life?

MARTIN'S POEM

The weekend had arrived at last! Some weeks at school seemed never-ending, especially when you had to sit three tests, two of which would only result in a Four, and a Six in the third. And that was only because the stupid teachers hadn't explained things properly or had caught you copying. But it was now Friday afternoon, and school could be forgotten about for two whole days.

Maren had gone to her Gran's for the weekend, and for the past three weeks Ina had been spending all her time with her new boyfriend.

'Doesn't he look gorgeous? And I'm his first girlfriend,' she constantly warbled on.

'If you believe that, you'll believe anything!' Rebekka thought. She'd seen Ina's heart-throb with at least three different girls in town. But she didn't want to spoil her romance. At least, she was certainly his latest girlfriend. Rebekka couldn't count on her at the moment.

So she went over to Martin's. Over recent weeks she'd begun to prefer spending time with him. She couldn't do anything mind-blowing when he was around, but at least he listened to her when she spoke about things.

And she could talk to him about serious issues, like death for instance. She couldn't do that with Maren, who seemed to be going through a "Let's be as silly as possible" phase at the moment, and was always killing herself laughing about everything. After a couple of sentences, Ina's conversation would always degenerate into a hymn of praise about her boyfriend. It was really amazing how a topic like "Why you can't leave Jelly Bears overnight on a radiator in the winter time" changed in three sentences into the conclusion, "My boyfriend is the best looking guy in the whole school including the teachers." Rebekka disagreed with her on this point. Compared to Herr Becker, Ina's boyfriend was a real wimp.

Sven opened the door.

'Hi, is Martin in?'

'Yes, come on in.'

Rebekka made a beeline for Martin's room. As she came in, she noticed that he was hurriedly shoving a notebook into a drawer.

'Hi, mate! What are you up to?'

'Nothing in particular,' he replied defensively.

She had the impression that she'd caught him doing something which he felt embarrassed about. It was just like that time when Mum had caught her reading a fairly - well, to be honest - a very dodgy magazine. She wondered what Martin had been up to. Had he been writing love letters? He certainly wouldn't read doubtful magazines. She wanted to find out more.

'What have you just hidden away?' She asked.

'Oh, nothing important,' Martin answered.

'What was it then?' Rebekka insisted.

She could be very persistent when she wanted to be.

'Just a poem I wrote.' Martin eventually gave in. He knew Rebekka would keep on and on until he told her.

'What - you write poetry? Let's see!'

Martin apparently had talents that she'd no idea he possessed. He admitted that he was beaten and pulled several pieces of paper out of the drawer. Rebekka grabbed them unceremoniously out of his hand.

'A love poem - eh?'

'Rubbish - it's not a love poem. You won't like it at all.' Martin was finding the whole thing very unpleasant. He stared at the floor or at the other side of the room in embarrassment. Rebekka began to read:

Without you, my God,
I'm like dust in the wind,
I'm like a lost child,
who's far from home.
Without you, my God,
my life is dead and empty.
I don't have any joy,
Lord, I need you!
Without you, my God,
my life would have no meaning,
I would wander about
with no goal,

'Martin, you lied to me!'

'What do you mean?' Martin looked at Rebekka in surprise.

'You said it wasn't love poetry, but I've never read anything like this before, where somebody is writing about needing someone so much. It is a love poem - to God!'

Rebekka wished with all her heart that she could get such fervent letters from Herr Becker. On the other hand, it was incredible that someone could be so enthusiastic about God although he'd never even seen him.

Martin smiled, looking embarrassed.

'You're probably right.'

Rebekka continued reading:

'Yet with you, my God,
my life has a purpose,
because I'm valuable to you,
and you can use me.
Yes, with you, my God,
I have hope and a goal,
you give me so much!
Lord, I need you!

Father, my God,
May people see you in me,
and know that you want to walk with them,
because you love them endlessly!
Yes, let me, my God,
live out - in the world -
your love which keeps me!
Lord, use me!

God means everything to you, doesn't he? I really don't get it. Why do people worship him? Don't you think you're exaggerating a bit?'

Martin said nothing for a while. Then he looked at her and said, 'Look, I'll try to explain it. Imagine you were totally broke and had 40,000 Marks worth of debts. You've had to sell your TV, your stereo, everything that was of value in your home.'

Rebekka wondered what this story had to do with her question, but she let Martin continue.

'You know that you have to pay back the cash you've borrowed in a fortnight's time, otherwise the outlook is grim - you can imagine. Then the postman arrives, bringing you a letter from a rich uncle in America.'

'I don't have an uncle in America,' Rebekka interrupted.

'Just imagine that you do! So, this fellow sends you a cheque for more than 2,000,000 dollars, because you're his favourite niece!'

Rebekka couldn't help grinning. She was more like every uncle's nightmare than a favourite niece.

'So then,' Martin continued, 'you take the cheque, hang it above your bed and let it gather dust. You don't throw it away though, perhaps you'll need it some time.'

'So you think I'm mad or something?' Rebekka shouted indignantly.

'Let me finish, please!' Martin pleaded. 'So the cheque is gathering dust, while you've hardly got anything to eat. A fortnight later, two thugs turn up and demand the money you owe. But you don't give them the money and they beat you up and kill you. End of story.'

Rebekka stared at him, feeling a bit confused. What did all that rubbish mean?

'Can you let me in on why you're speaking such rubbish? Nobody's as dumb as that! I'm certainly not!'

'It's meant to be an illustration. This is the way I think of it: everybody has run up debts in his life - which they owe to other people and to God. Sort of being in debt to God - that's the money. We can't pay them off ourselves. That's why we've really no hope.'

'Yes, but the cheque?'

'Exactly - the cheque. Jesus paid our debts with his life and offers us friendship with God - that's the cheque. This cheque doesn't only cover our debts, but it also makes possible a completely new life with God. God loves us and has something great planned for each person, I'm sure about that. It's up to us whether we accept this offer or choose to continue with our old life - letting the cheque gather dust and dying as a result.'

Rebekka stared at the floor, deep in thought. Could things really be as extreme as that? She didn't feel particularly guilty.

'I don't know - isn't that a bit over the top? I mean, I don't think I'm really that bad.'

'I'm as bad as that,' Martin countered. 'But I decided to accept the cheque. It's worth it! That's why I'm so enthusiastic about God and Jesus. It's fantastic when you don't have to cope alone with the things that you make a mess of, not to mention your worries and problems. You know that there's someone who has it all under control and who loves you, in spite of all your faults. I don't think my poem was an exaggeration.'

Rebekka had to smile. When Martin enthused about God like that, you could almost believe that being a Christian was really cool. But only for Martin. She didn't need God and she didn't need a friendship with Jesus. Her life was okay the way it was. Definitely.

A GREAT PLAN

There were only two more weeks to go before the start of the summer holidays. Nobody was taking things very seriously at school - that included both teachers and pupils. It was the time of year when the occasional joke could be played without the teachers blowing their tops. Martin had a brainwave. During break time he, Rebekka, Sascha and Timo sneaked along to the teachers' car park, which was near the street, so that all the parked cars could easily be seen. As inconspicuously as possible, the four of them stuck notices, which they'd designed on the computer, behind the windscreen wipers of several cars. On one of the posters the following words were clearly visible:

FOR SALE: Because of excessive debts, marital troubles and other problems the car is up for immediate sale for 2,567 Marks (cash).
Year of construction: 1973
Special feature: has been relatively free from accidents. If interested, please make enquiries at the staffroom in Wilhelm-Busch School.

Sascha and Timo had found three old street cordons in a ditch, and they had placed these around Herr Merten's car as well. Now it really looked like the car was ready to be towed away to the scrapyard.

After the deed had been done the four sneaked back into the playground. They couldn't help looking forward to seeing the flabbergasted expression on Herr Merten's face, because he took such a pride in his Mercedes.

They didn't need to wait long for the initial reaction. During the next lesson Herr Mertens came in. His face was bright red and he looked extremely irritated. In his hand he held the shameful piece of paper as evidence of the wanton act which someone had perpetrated in valuing his wonderful Mercedes at the ridiculous amount of only 2,500 Marks!

'Who stuck this sign on my Mercedes?' He shouted indignantly. 'A man has just come into the staffroom asking if he could get 'the old wreck' for a mere 2,500 My Mercedes for 2,500 Marks. What a cheek!'

The class snorted with laughter. At long last, the man had discovered what his dream car was really worth. Herr Mertens looked furiously at them.

'It's no laughing matter!' He yelled, flushed with anger. Then he left the classroom at double-speed.

'Do you think God enjoys your jokes?' Rebekka asked Martin, after everything had calmed down a bit.

'I think so. God certainly has a sense of humour. I think He uses humour sometimes to correct people's blindspots,' Martin grinned. 'In Merten's case his car meant everything to him. Maybe he's realised now that others don't view it in quite the same way.'

Most of the teachers were in a very good mood just

before the holidays. Some told stories, gave them puzzles to do or nicer things like that. At times like these school was actually bearable. However, Rebekka would have preferred to have no lessons at all. The only thing that cast a shadow over the holidays was the thought that she wouldn't be able to see Herr Becker for six long weeks. How could she survive? But otherwise, the holidays were a really welcome break after such a stressful year at school.

This year she'd be going once again with her parents to Aunt Marta's on the Baltic coast. Rebekka liked the sea considerably more than her Aunt. In addition to the aforementioned lady, there was a fat, usually sullen Uncle, a terribly conceited cousin called Birgit, and an irritating little cousin by the name of Marcel. Her relatives were an annoying but inevitable intrusion on the holiday. Nevertheless, Rebekka always looked forward to this holiday, because the long walks on the beach made up for all the hassle with her relatives.

'What are you going to do over the holidays?' She asked Martin.

'Oh, nothing special. I'll probably paint a bit, play computer games, and maybe go around on my moped. That's of course if my parents give me some money on my birthday, then I'll be able to buy a second-hand one.'

Martin had obtained his moped licence about two weeks previously. Riding a bike would have tired him out too much, so he would be a lot more independent and mobile if he had a moped.

'I'm sure your parents will do that for you. When is your birthday as a matter of fact?' Rebekka wanted to know.

'This Friday.'

Rebekka couldn't remember receiving an invitation, and asked, 'So, who are you inviting?'

'No-one. I'm not having a party,' Martin replied.

'What do you mean - you're not going to do anything special at all?'

Martin shook his head.

'Why not?' Rebekka couldn't imagine a birthday without a party and lots of people around.

'Eh, I wouldn't be able to do anything exciting. I can't dance or do anything like that. I'm sure other people wouldn't enjoy sitting around and talking for hours on end. I wouldn't know who to invite anyway. I don't think anyone would be very keen to come along especially for my birthday.'

Rebekka was horrified. Birthdays were for celebrating!

'You're not going to do anything special at all on your birthday?'

'Oh yes,' Martin reassured her, 'my mother usually cooks my favourite meal. I hope to get presents and I can please myself how I spend the day. I might go and see a film with Sven.'

Somehow Rebekka felt sad that Martin wasn't going to celebrate properly. Someone had to do something about it. Suddenly she had an idea. Why couldn't she give Martin a surprise party? Her parents didn't mind how she spent her money. She was determined to organise something - secretly of course! She would only take Sven and Frau Baumann into her confidence - maybe they would have some good suggestions too.

In history, Herr Krom told them the same old story

for the twelfth time about how a pupil had actually fallen asleep during his teaching practice. What was so unusual about that? Rebekka wasn't listening any more. She was trying to work out how a birthday party could be laid on for Martin. It would be great if he could have a lot of people along. Rebekka looked around her - who could she invite? She knew at least one person she would definitely not invite - that complete idiot Kai! Stefan, Sascha, and Timo would definitely come and Maren, Sebastian, Anne and Mark. Ina would probably prefer to be with her new boyfriend, who was apparently even better looking than her ex. She'd already dropped that creep after four weeks because he was crude and boring. Oliver was actually quite nice, if only he didn't tell his stupid jokes all the time.

'I have an appointment at the university clinic tomorrow,' Martin remarked at break time. 'They want to measure me and we'll probably get to speak to the surgeon who'll be doing the transplant operation. Maybe I'll get onto the waiting list soon after that.'

'Wow, that's just great!' Rebekka said, 'then it could happen soon!'

By this time Rebekka could think of the transplant operation in a more positive light, and she was trying to get rid of her fears about it going wrong.

In the last couple of months Martin's condition appeared to be deteriorating. The slightest thing caused him to get out of breath, and it was probably only a matter of time before he'd no longer be able to come to school. The distance between classrooms and departments was just too much for him. But Rebekka had other reasons for being pleased that Martin wouldn't be at home the following day. It would give her time to discuss the idea about a birthday party with Sven, without Martin finding out about it.

The next day Rebekka phoned the Baumanns just after lunch. As she'd expected, Sven answered the phone.

'It's good that I've caught you in,' she babbled, 'I have to talk to you about something. It's very important!'

'You want to speak to me?' Sven was surprised. 'What about?'

'I'll tell you later. Can I come over?'

'I'm in the middle of writing a report.'

Sven was at technical college.

'But if it's so important, just come over. Martin isn't here, you know. He's away at his appointment.'

'That's excellent,' Rebekka replied. 'See you in a few minutes!'

Rebekka had hung up before a baffled Sven could even ask what was so good about having a hospital appointment.

She hurriedly described her great idea to Sven - she wanted it to catch his imagination. He was very keen about the whole thing straightaway.

'Let's invite a few of his friends from the Young People's Meeting, then he'll be even more pleased.'

Rebekka didn't think much of that suggestion.

'Won't they be too . . . em sort of religious for the rest of the crowd?'

'You must be joking!' Sven laughed. 'They can be a really good laugh. They're an okay bunch, even you will like them!'

Rebekka doubted that very much. Martin had often asked her to come along to the YPM but she didn't want

67

to go to a Bible-reading, singing, playing-games club. One of the main reasons for not going was because Gran would have been over the moon as soon as she got wind of it. There was no way she was going to give the old woman that pleasure.

'Markus there, is really good at playing the guitar and Carmen plays the flute. We could even practice singing a birthday song for Martin,' Sven continued enthusiastically.

Rebekka thought that the idea wasn't too bad.

After an hour's discussion the plan took shape - they would invite everyone secretly to the ice- cream cafe round the corner. Markus could rehearse the birthday song with them there. While that was happening, Rebekka would turn up at Martin's house to wish him a happy birthday. He wouldn't have a clue about what was going to happen. She'd invite him "on the spur of the moment" to come and have an ice-cream. Martin loved ice-cream. Then, when he arrived at the cafe, everyone would burst into song. Rebekka and Sven were looking forward to seeing the flabbergasted expression on Martin's face.

'He'll be so surprised, he won't know what to say,' Sven said.

The two of them also sorted out the financial side of things - Sven, his mother and Rebekka would share the costs involved. Frau Baumann didn't actually know about her part in it yet, but she'd be sure to join in. It was all systems go!

THE SURPRISE

It had been ages since Rebekka had felt so excited.

'At this rate, I'll probably end up enjoying the birthday more than Martin himself!' She thought.

All the people she'd invited at school were willing to come along. Who could resist the offer of eating as much ice-cream as they wanted for free? A few of them had even clubbed together to get a present for Martin. They thought it would be best if it was something unusual so that he'd be reminded of the day for a long time afterwards. Of course, all the arrangements had to be made without Martin suspecting anything. But somehow Rebekka managed to slip little notes to the other people in their classes without Martin spotting what she was doing.

At long last the time had arrived. According to the plan, everyone would meet up at the ice-cream place at 5 o'clock. Sven had reserved three tables for them in advance. The people from the YPM were there complete with guitar and flute ready to practise singing "Happy Birthday." Amazingly enough, everyone had actually arrived on time, even Anne, who was always usually at least ten minutes late. The ice-cream probably had something to do with it.

Rebekka looked into the doorway of the cafe as she passed by on her way to Martin's. She had pictured the YPM people quite differently - somehow more serious and reserved. Markus was playing his guitar and singing an impromptu song which he'd written, which didn't actually make sense, but that only made it all the funnier. There was a relaxed and happy atmosphere. Rebekka was almost sorry that she had to leave and go round to Martin's, but on the other hand, she was looking forward even more to surprising him.

She walked along to the Baumanns' house, carrying her present (a joke book about teachers), and practising a little speech in her head.

'It's such fantastic weather - let's go and have an ice-cream. I'll treat you.'

It was Martin who answered the door. Nobody rang doorbells as enthusiastically as Rebekka, especially when she was excited about something.

'My warmest congratulations - old pal! I hope that you'll reach the age of 187 one day!'

Martin laughed, 'I'll try hard to do that! Thanks very much! Come in!'

'I've got a better idea. Why don't we go and have an ice-cream? I'll treat you! It's such a lovely day today.'

Rebekka had scarcely finished her sentence when it began to drizzle. What a pain! Why did it always have to rain at the most inconvenient of times?'

'Oh, I don't know,' Martin said, 'I'm not really in the mood. It would be nicer to stay and eat some ice-cream here. My mother has some in the freezer.'

Rebekka struggled not to give away the surprise.

'Please, Martin,' she begged. 'I'd really like to treat you to something today. Go on, do me the favour!'

'Oh yes!' insisted Martin's mother, who had joined them by now, 'I think it's a great idea too. Go out and have an ice-cream. I've only got one flavour here at home and you could get yourself a strawberry sundae there. Have a good time! Maybe Sven wants to go as well - Sven!'

Sven came bounding along right away. He'd been standing waiting behind his bedroom door.

'Yes?' he asked innocently.

'Do you want to go to the cafe with Rebekka and Martin?'

'Of course, if I'm allowed to!'

Martin looked questioningly at his mother. He couldn't get out of it now. He had to go for an ice- cream with the other two. He set off with them rather reluctantly. Rebekka was worried in case she might have spoiled the day for him. But she needn't have worried.

When they arrived at the cafe, everyone stood up and sang Happy Birthday.

Rebekka had never seen Martin look so taken aback before and yet so happy. She noticed that he was swallowing hard occasionally. When everyone had shouted out 'Happy Birthday!' He could hardly say a word.

'I'm really gobsmacked!' He stammered eventually.

He couldn't continue because he was inundated with presents from all directions. There were some very original things - a handmade paper basket, covered with photos of his friends from the YPM, an inflatable plastic birthday cake from his classmates, a giant 'bouquet' of sweets from Maren, Anne and Rebekka, and a desk-tidy, which resembled a tiny set of panpipes, from Sven. Everyone had made an incredible effort. Martin didn't know what to look at first. He kept shaking his head in disbelief and muttering now and then, 'I'm really stunned!' And 'I don't know what to say!' He didn't need to say anything because it was obvious to everyone that the surprise had been a success. Rebekka felt deeply satisfied and as happy as Martin. It was simply cool to spring a surprise on someone like that. It would be good to do things like that more often.

After the initial excitement, even Martin's, had subsided a bit, they all sat down and ordered ice-creams. While they were waiting for them to arrive, Markus began to sing a song which some of the YPM joined in with. The words were about Jesus, and Martin sang along heartily as well. His classmates looked a bit shocked at first but then apparently seemed to find the music quite good. Some of them even tried to sing along. Even Rebekka thought the music wasn't bad. It sounded so different from what was normally sung in church. Besides, these Christians here were a lot more cheerful than the old ladies in her church. Before her confirmation she'd had to go to church on Sundays. It was a silly institution and deadly boring!

Eventually, the ice-cream arrived and everyone tucked in. Martin was still grinning from ear to ear and he seemed to be on a real high. He was sitting at a table with his YPM friends, and Rebekka was sitting next to him.

'Tell me, Bekki,' he eventually asked, 'did you know about this?'

'Of course,' grinned Rebekka, 'it was my idea!'

Martin looked at her in disbelief.

'You hatched the whole thing?'

She nodded.

'I know you can be quite nice sometimes, but I'd never have guessed you were such a gem!'

Once again Rebekka could have easily been mistaken for a railway signal because she turned such a shade of red. Luckily, the others were so engrossed in their conversations that they didn't notice. Only Martin grinned with a knowing look on his face.

When everyone had finished their first helping of ice-cream, Maja, a girl from the YPM had a suggestion to make. She came over to Martin and asked quietly, 'Do you want to try one of the sketches?'

Markus overheard her suggestion and was all for it, 'Oh yes, that would be really good - it'll give us time to digest our ice-cream!'

At first Martin needed a lot of persuading, but as soon as his classmates realised that he could act out sketches, they all pestered and nagged him for ages until he gave in. He was really good at acting. It was really hilarious to watch Maja (who towered above him) and Martin pretending to be 'an old married couple.'

'Just when you think you know someone, they surprise you. I wonder what other talents Martin has that I haven't a clue about?' Rebekka thought. Of course, one sketch was not enough. The first one had hardly finished when Martin's YPM friends applauded and demanded an encore. Apparently, they knew that he had more up his sleeve. Martin acted out three more sketches, sometimes with Maja who could also act very well, and sometimes on his own. He really seemed to come to life, as he stood there playing the part of either a husband, a lottery winner or an angry father. And strangely enough, it didn't seem to tire him out at all.

After the sketches were finished, they all had a second helping of ice-cream. After all, they might as well make the most of their invitation! Then Carmen played a lovely piece of music on her flute. Even Rebekka liked it, although she listened to very little music apart from hard rock. Some of these religious people seemed to be very talented.

Eventually, a rather well built boy stood up and sang a song which he'd composed about his apprenticeship. It was really hilarious and Rebekka wondered when she'd last had so much fun. She couldn't remember.

It was now almost eight o'clock and they were still sitting in the cafe. Its owner seemed to enjoy watching the happy crowd of young people. He certainly didn't have customers like that every day.

'I think we should begin to make tracks,' Markus said, 'we could continue over in my house.'

The idea was unanimously accepted, or to be more accurate, only Sascha, Anne, Timo and Oliver had to go home then.

Once they'd arrived at the Baumanns' house, they all sat down in the large sitting room.

'Do you want to play a game?' Markus asked.

'Oh no,' Rebekka thought, 'we're going to get kids' stuff now!'

Everyone else seemed enthusiastic about the suggestion.

'We could play Baptists' skat or the dictionary game,'

Martin suggested.

'Baptists' skat? Dictionary game? What kind of weird games are they?' thought Rebekka. She was only familiar with things like ludo, draughts, snakes and ladders and that was about the limit of her repetoire of games.

The majority wanted to play Baptists' skat. Someone explained the game briefly and then it started. It only took two rounds for Rebekka to get hooked. She would have liked to play it all evening but after an hour the others wanted to play the dictionary game for a change. This was quite appealing too, as Rebekka soon discovered. What surprised her most was how happy the people from the YPM were. They were a really nice bunch. Perhaps she should think about going to their meetings. They couldn't be all that bad, because the people were so funny.

At about ten o'clock, most of the guests left and thanked everyone once again for the party.

Martin thanked Rebekka effusively, 'That was the best idea you've ever had! You really succeeded in surprising me!'

'You surprised me too,' Rebekka replied. 'I'd no idea that you were an actor. I'm interested to know what other hidden talents you have!'

'Oh, I'm not that brilliant. But today was really the best birthday that I can remember. Thank you, Bekki!'

'It's okay. I enjoyed it too. See you tomorrow!'

And with that she was gone.

A JUMP START

The holiday had to be cancelled - what a huge disappointment. A couple of days before the summer holidays began, Aunt Marta phoned up and reported that Birgit and Marcel had caught the measles. Rebekka hadn't had the measles, so the holiday was out. It was true that they could have gone on holiday somewhere else, but it wouldn't have been as nice as the Baltic coast. Dad only commented that this suited him, because he had so much to do, he didn't know where to start.

What a downer! How could she spend six long weeks at home? Even the weather wasn't on Rebekka's side. It rained constantly and was also fairly cold. You would have thought it was either April or you were living in Britain. When they'd been over there on holiday once, it had rained twice during the week - the first time for three days and the second time it had gone on for four days! That country should really have a huge roof built over it!

Almost everyone had gone away except Martin. But he was always out and about on his moped, which he'd bought with the money he'd had for his birthday. He didn't seem to bother about the rain.

It was really totally boring. Everyone else was spending time on a beach in Mallorca or Denmark. Ina had gone on a camping trip with boyfriend number three. This bloke was 19 and, according to Ina, was really the most gorgeous male in the whole world. Rebekka thought that he looked a bit like Kermit the Frog.

Even Daniel was away with his girlfriend - he'd been going out with her for about three years now. As the Baltic holiday had fallen through, they'd decided to go for a short break to Frankfurt to see one of her friends. Only Rebekka was left, hanging around at home and feeling lonely and deserted. It really wasn't fair. What was the point of having holidays if you couldn't get the benefit from them?

She wondered if Herr Becker was at home. Just one week of the holidays had gone by, but Rebekka was already pining for him. Why had she been daft enough to fall for a teacher of all people? She could kick herself. She really felt like phoning him. But what could she say to him - 'Hello, Herr Becker, I miss you!' She could hardly say something like that!

If only they'd been given some English homework to do over the holidays! That was certainly a weird thing to wish for someone who detested school. She could have asked him questions about it. But they never usually got homework to do over the summer. Then Rebekka had an idea. She could simply say, 'Oh, I must have dialled the wrong number by mistake. I'm sorry. You're not away on holiday, then?' And then she'd be able to have a conversation with him - just between the two of them.

Rebekka felt very nervous at the thought of being able to speak to the guy. Impulsively, she picked up the phone, dialled the number which she'd memorised ages ago, and waited with bated breath in sheer excitement.

'Becker,' answered a woman's pleasant voice. That is to say, Rebekka only thought it was pleasant when she first heard it but later she felt annoyed at this silly woman. Rebekka lost her tongue in sheer fright.

'Frau Becker here. Who's calling, please?' The woman asked after a short pause, and Rebekka abruptly put the receiver down. What a disaster! Why did this man have to be married to a wife who apparently wouldn't even let him get to the phone! Rebekka sighed. What a terrible day!

She was just about to sit down in front of her TV because she didn't know what else to do, when she heard the sound of Martin's moped. A second later, the bell rang. Rebekka met him at the door. He was beaming as if someone had just handed him a giant chocolate cake.

'Hey, Bekki! Look what I've got here!' He said, and waved a small object which resembled an electric shaver under her nose.

'What's that?' Rebekka asked, irritably.

'It's my bleeper!' Martin explained. He was bubbling over with enthusiasm.

'It's great, isn't it? It means that I'm on the waiting list for the heart and lung transplant operation at last!'

'Wow! That's great!' Rebekka became enthusiastic now too. 'How does the thing work?'

'It's quite simple. When they page me, the device makes a certain sound and a small light appears on the display here. Then I'll know that I have to phone right away. When the battery's done, the thing will bleep too, but it'll make a different sound. And if I want to know if it's still working, I only need to switch it off and back on once, and it'll make the same sound as if they were paging me. It's cool, isn't it?'

Martin was as delighted with his bleeper as Rebekka had been with her CD player.

'I can even attach the thing to the front of my moped,' Martin continued. 'My mother and I have already tested it out. It works perfectly.'

'So you're really on the waiting list now, and it can happen at any time?'

'Exactly!'

'How long could it take until it's your turn?'

'You just never know. In theory it could happen tonight, but it might take another two years.'

'Two years?' Rebekka couldn't help remembering that the doctors had told Martin that without a transplant operation he would only live for another two years at most. Was there a possibility that he wouldn't make it? She didn't want to think about it.

'Let's hear your pager bleeping then!' She said. 'Then I'll recognise the signal too.'

Martin switched the pager off and then on again. An ear-splitting bleeping tone immediately sounded, as Rebekka discovered. She felt a bit queasy at the thought that the thing could go off at any moment and Martin would be taken away for his weird operation. She couldn't imagine it at all, especially the bit about the new organs.

'Are you free just now?' She asked eventually, in order to change the subject.

'Of course. Any ideas about what we can do?'

'We could have a game of Pope's skat or whatever you call it? I really enjoyed playing that.'

Martin agreed right away. He enjoyed playing it too. Soon they were engrossed in their game. Only from time to time Rebekka glanced at the pager which Martin had placed on the table in front of him. What if it suddenly went off? What were they supposed to do then? They'd have to phone up Martin's house, that was obvious enough, but what would happen after that?

Somehow Rebekka felt quite tense. She couldn't concentrate properly on the game. Martin seemed to be having a similar problem. Although Baptists' skat was a straightforward card game, he kept asking, 'Where have you put the dice?' Or else he'd wait for ages and then ask, sounding a bit confused, 'Is it my turn again?'

Each time this happened Rebekka grinned to herself. 'Hey, have you actually got their phone number, in case you have to phone them?'

'Of course. I've stuck it onto the back of the pager.' Rebekka breathed a sigh of relief. In that case nothing could go wrong if it started to bleep.

After three hours of card games (even a month before this Rebekka would have thought that anyone spending so long playing games was crazy), Martin had a brilliant idea.

'Do you know what, we should really celebrate getting onto the waiting list at last! How about going out for a meal? It'll be on me - a sort of small "Thank you" for the great birthday party.'

Rebekka was immediately in favour of that. She didn't usually get invited out for meals and was always keen where food was concerned. You could tell that simply by looking at her.

'And how will we get to the restaurant?'

'That's no problem,' Martin explained. 'Sven will be going over to Markus's later on anyway. They're planning what to do at the YPM on Friday. Markus lives near the Greek restaurant. Sven'll take us along there. Do you like Greek food?'

What a question! Nothing could beat Gyros and coleslaw!

Half an hour later they were sitting in Sven's car.

'What are you planning to do this Friday?' Rebekka asked him.

'The theme's going to be 'God can wait!'' Sven informed her, 'It's about the father in the story of the lost son.'

Lost son? She'd never heard of it, but it sounded intriguing. Perhaps someone had lost their toddler in a store or something like that. It would perhaps be okay to go to this club after all.

'What time does your meeting start?'

'Half seven. Shall I come and pick you up?'

Sven seemed to have read her thoughts. How did he know that she wanted to go along?

'Em . . . Well, okay. I'll wait outside my house for you.' Rebekka said.

Sven beamed. He seemed to be genuinely pleased that she wanted to come along, and Martin obviously felt the same because he was grinning happily at her too.

The car had arrived at the restaurant by this time, and they thanked Sven before going inside. They found a comfortable corner to themselves, and were just about to have a good look at the menu when a familiar bleeping sound disturbed them. Rebekka nearly jumped off her chair in fright.

'That's your pager!' She shouted in such a loud, agitated state that every person in the restaurant could hear her.

Martin immediately fished the gadget out of his jacket pocket.

'I can't see anything on the display though!'

'Then it must be broken,' Rebekka's heart was beating so hard, she thought it would burst.

They heard the bleeping sound once more, and Martin stared at the display again. He couldn't see anything on it at all.

'Maybe the noise is coming from the till. Doesn't it sound a bit different from my pager?' He concluded.

'We can test that out easily enough. Switch the thing off and on again!'

Martin tried and it was the same sound as they'd already heard twice.

'I'll phone home and find out if the clinic has called. They'll phone my house before they page me in any case.' Martin got up slowly and walked over to the cashier. There he heard the bleeping sound again but this time it was even louder. He wondered if it was coming from the till.

'Can I make a short telephone call, please? It's quite urgent.'

The waiter let him use the phone right away.

Rebekka sat at the table, waiting. It was more nail-biting than watching a crime thriller. Eventually, Martin returned, smiling. 'Everything's okay,' he reassured her. 'Nobody has phoned our house in the last half hour. It must have been the till that we heard.'

Rebekka heaved a sigh of relief. At last they could eat their meal in peace. She needed a double portion of gyros and coleslaw to recover from the shock. Once they were tucking into their meal, everything felt alright again and it was okay to laugh about the whole incident.

After the meal they went for a short stroll, enjoying the mild evening air.

'If your gadget bleeps again, it'll give me a heart attack!' Rebekka laughed.

She'd hardly finished her sentence when the bleeping started again.

'Martin!' She screamed, feeling terrified.

But he only grinned, and said, as calm as cucumber, 'Just joking! I switched the pager off and on.'

Rebekka couldn't see the funny side of it at all. 'Sometimes, you're really the limit!' She yelled.

But Martin looked at her with such an innocent expression on his face that she couldn't be angry with him.

'You dingbat!' She said eventually, and began to laugh as well.

A REALLY
BRILLIANT FATHER

The tension caused by the pager was slowly beginning to subside and now they no longer expected every phone call to be about the transplant operation. Over the first few days they had been startled every time the phone rang. If they happened to be in his room, Martin would look for his case, which had been packed ages ago for his hospital stay. Sometimes Martin and Rebekka would speculate about who the donor might be. Would he be about their age? Or would he be a young Dad?

'Sometimes I imagine that he'll have to die specially for me, and I feel that I don't really deserve that,' Martin said at one point.

'Rubbish!' Rebekka interrupted. 'They're not going to kill anyone just so that you can get their organs. The donor will already be dead!'

'Just recently I read in the paper that a tourist had been found murdered, and his heart and kidneys had been cut out. I really wouldn't want to have organs that had been taken like that!' Martin insisted.

'I don't think that you need to worry about something like that happening. Of course rotten characters who trade in organs do exist, but I read in a health insurance magazine that two doctors, who are not part of the transplant team, have to make sure that the person is brain dead before they're allowed to remove any organs. And if someone's brain dead, then there's no way they can be brought back to life again.'

'As far as I know, it's illegal to pay money for organs, here in Germany. The reason why these butchers can still sell so many on the black market is that there are too few donors. I suppose there aren't enough of them, partly because of all the horror stories that are spread about people trading in organs, and tourists being cut open. It's a vicious circle!'

'You could be right there,' Rebekka agreed with him, 'That's why I'm carrying an organ donor card around with me now!'

She proudly showed Martin the little card. Perhaps she might be able to help someone like him one day by donating an organ. You just never knew.

It was really excellent that Martin hadn't gone away on holiday, so Rebekka had at least one person she could spend time with. It was true that they couldn't go cycling or take a stroll into town, but they could play games, chat and go to see films.

'Tell me something, if I come along to your young people's meeting on Friday, do I have to do something there or take anything with me?' Rebekka asked.

You just never knew about these things. Perhaps there would be certain rituals she'd have to go through. The first time she'd gone to church, no one had explained to her what happened, and she'd felt really dumb during the first few minutes. People had constantly stood up and sat down, and had all sung something incomprehensible in response to the pastor - "Curry, yeah! Ellie Son!' or something like that.

She had wondered despairingly how they all knew what to sing. Were they reading it from something? And then they had sung really ancient songs. She didn't even have a song book and hadn't known what was happening or why. She didn't want to land up in a similar situation again.

'You don't need to bring anything with you to the YPM. Just come as you are. All you have to do is to introduce yourself briefly. Then all you'll have to say is what your name is, your age, where you live and stuff like that. We just sit around and talk, sing and play games. It's very laid back. You know several of the bunch now anyway.'

Rebekka felt more reassured. Besides, Martin would be there as well. Over the last few days she'd begun to look forward to the YPM or whatever they called it.

'Martin, you must promise me one thing . . .'

'What?'

'If you bump into my Gran, don't you dare tell her that I was at your YPM, okay?'

'It's a deal. But why?' He enquired.

'She just doesn't need to know,' Rebekka evaded his question. Perhaps Martin would have no time for the fact that she didn't want to give her Gran that pleasure. He just looked at her blankly, but didn't ask any more questions.

On Friday, Sven and Martin came to Rebekka's house bang on quarter past seven to pick her up. As she'd forgotten to ask Martin about what kind of thing she should wear, she had put on her newest pair of jeans and a fashionable jumper. Her mother had told her to put on some decent clothes.

There were already several people waiting outside the building where they all usually met. Carmen and some others whom Rebekka recognised from the birthday party were there and they gave her an enthusiastic welcome.

'Hi! Great to see you here! Your name's Rebekka, right? I hope you'll enjoy it. Markus has just gone to get the key from our pastor. How are you at table tennis?'

'Actually it's tennis I usually play. Why?'

'We usually play table tennis for a few minutes before the meeting starts. None of us are pros though, so you can easily join in.' Carmen winked at her. 'It's definitely time that us girls got in some more troops to help us!'

Rebekka felt completely accepted and on top of the world. Carmen and the other girls there seemed to be okay, really. Markus came running up, his guitar (his trademark!) in one hand, and the key in the other.

The table tennis table went up as soon as they got inside. Rebekka looked around. She liked the room - it had large windows, vases of flowers, and on one wall there were lots of pictures which had obviously been painted by young kids. They looked really funny.

'Who painted these pictures? You lot certainly didn't do them - did you?'

'No,' Martin explained. 'It was the little tots who did those - that's the three to six year olds. On Monday afternoons they have a group. Carmen and Ulrike organise it.'

'And what do they do there?'

'Play games, tell stories, paint, do crafts, and stuff like that, I think. You should ask them about it.'

Rebekka took a closer look at the pictures. Some of them looked very cute. A little boy called Kevin, (you could read his name in the right hand corner) had painted a little stick man wearing an enormous walkman, and scribbled beside it, 'Jesus heers eveyting.' Rebekka couldn't help laughing. She had her doubts about Jesus listening to a Walkman! One little girl had drawn masses of brightly coloured little figures beside a larger figure and written above it 'Jesus lisens to everywun.' It referred to the story that the children had heard earlier.

Eventually Markus shouted 'Come on, let's get started!'

Gradually, everyone came and sat down in chairs which were set out in a circle. Rebekka was glad she'd escaped playing table tennis. She might have made a fool of herself.

There were about twenty people there, and when they were all seated and it gradually grew a bit quieter, Markus welcomed Rebekka .

'Some of us met you at Martin's great birthday party. Now I can let the secret out - Rebekka arranged the whole thing.'

Some of the others gave her a burst of applause and looked at her approvingly.

Rebekka turned as red as beetroot.

'But perhaps it would be best if you introduced yourself,' Markus suggested.

Rebekka looked at Martin. He smiled at her as if to say, 'Don't panic - they're not going to bite!'

'Well,' Rebekka began 'I'm Rebekka Jansen, I'm

fifteen, and live near Martin. Em... I'm still at school, single,' some saw the funny side of that and chuckled, 'I've got an older brother. What else do you want to know?'

'I think that'll do for now,' Markus said. Before they started the Bible study, they sang a few songs which Rebekka actually liked, not always because of the words - there were a lot she didn't understand, but the melodies and rhythms were quite passable.

After about four songs, Bibles were handed out. Rebekka received a small blue one. It was a handier size than the one she'd had from Gran but it wasn't in such good condition.

'Let's look up Luke 15, verses 11 to 24!'

'Where in the world was that in this thick book?' Rebekka thought. The others seemed to have found the place ages ago, while Rebekka was still scanning the contents page.

'I don't have a Luke or whatever it is in my book,' she whispered to the girl sitting next to her.

Her neighbour smiled and showed her where she could find it.

'But it says there *The Gospel According to Luke!* And it doesn't mention a 15 at all,' Rebekka thought to herself.

The girl took her Bible and opened it at the right place. It was only then that Rebekka realised that everyone else had been waiting and she felt quite embarrassed about it.

'I must look like a right idiot,' she thought.

'I think it'd be best if we all read the passage through by ourselves, before discussing it,' Markus said, and everyone started to read.

'Jesus went on to say, "There was once a man who had two sons. The younger one said to him, 'Father, give me my share of the property now.' So the man divided his property between his two sons. After a few days the younger son sold his part of the property and left home with the money. He went to a country far away, where he wasted his money in reckless living. He spent everything he had."'

Rebekka tried hard to imagine how her father would react if she went to him and said, 'Dad, do me a favour, and give me the dosh I'd be due if you'd died.' He would not be too happy about that. Rebekka was sure there'd either be a mega row or Dad would suffer a heart attack. There was no way he'd dish out the money to her.

What about the father in this story? He didn't make a scene, there were no angry outbursts, or scathing remarks like 'Don't come running to me when it all goes wrong!' No, the man let his lout of a son go off with his inheritance. What kind of father was that? She was interested to find out what happened next. She'd never imagined there were such interesting stories in the Bible.

'He spent everything he had. Then a severe famine spread over that country, and he was left without a thing. So he went to work for one of the citizens of that country, who sent him out to his farm to take care of the pigs. He wished he could fill himself with the bean pods the pigs ate, but no one gave him anything to eat.'

'Serves him right,' Rebekka thought. First he squeezes money out of his old man and goes abroad and then he goes and blows the whole fortune. It was his own fault that he'd nothing to eat.

'At last he came to his senses and said, "All my father's hired workers have more than they can eat, and here I am about to starve! I will get up and go to my father and say, 'Father, I have sinned against God and against you. I am no longer fit to be called your son; treat me as one of your hired workers.'"

That just wasn't on! Now that he was at the end of his tether, he was going to go grovelling back to his Dad. 'If I was in that father's shoes, I'd chuck that nasty piece of work out of the house,' Rebekka thought.

'So he got up and started back to his father. He was still a long way from home when his father saw him; his heart was filled with pity and he ran, threw his arms round his son, and kissed him.

"Father," the son said, "I have sinned against God and against you. I am no longer fit to be called your son." But the father called his servants, "Hurry!" He said. "Bring the best robe and put it on him. Put a ring on his finger and shoes on his feet. Then go and get the prize calf and kill it, and let us celebrate with a feast! For this son of mine was dead, but now is alive; he was lost, but now he has been found. And so the feasting began.'"

Rebekka was taken aback. The last thing she'd expected was that the father would throw a party for that guy. This one was really extremely unusual - he was dead brilliant! In similar circumstances, her father would have thrown her out of the family. But what was the point of the story?

'This story really shows us what a good Father God is,' Sven began, after everyone had finished reading.

So the father in the story was meant to be God. Were all people really like this son, who made such an exhibition of himself, and then came grovelling back to his father? Rebekka struggled with this idea. Okay, she had her faults, but who didn't? But she was definitely not as rotten as that character.

'Even though the son in the story didn't want to have anything to do with his father, and frittered away everything, at the end of the story the father accepted him back and still loved him,' Sven continued.

"Often we don't want to have anything to do with God. Lots of people run away from him deliberately and want to live their own lives. In doing so, they often waste everything God has given them - their talents, time and their lives'

Rebekka felt as if Sven was speaking just to her. Had she really run away like the boy in the story? Had she squandered what the Father had given her?

'Just like the Father in this story, God waits for each person to come back to him. He doesn't force himself into our lives. The father in our story could have forced his son to stay at home, or he could have searched everywhere for him and brought him home. But that's not God's way. God waits. Because he loves us so much, and because he wants us to choose to come to him. He longs for us constantly, but he'll never force us to live with him. God waits until the son, or the daughter, comes to him, and that's the best place for him or her to be.'

Sven continued speaking but Rebekka didn't hear any more. She kept thinking about what Sven had said about the waiting Father. If God was really this Father who was waiting and if it was really good for people to be with him, shouldn't she try it out?

IT CAN'T GO ON LIKE THIS!

Rebekka had turned things over in her mind for ages after the evening at the YPM, and she felt torn in two. She was drawn to God, to this Father who loved her, was waiting for her, and who always had time for her, just as Jesus had described it in the story. It felt as if all her doubts had been swept away. The story about the guy who ran away, had blown everything he had, and then been accepted back again with such love, Sven's words and everything Martin had talked to her about before, kept going round in her mind. She began to long more and more to get to know this good God. But was it all really as simple as it sounded?

'Martin, suppose I wanted to become a Christian, what exactly would I have to do?' She asked her best friend, after struggling with this question for four days.

'Do you remember the story about the boy who ran away from home?'

Sure, that was what had made her feel restless in the first place.

'You just need to speak to God, like the son spoke to his father. Admit to him what you think you've done wrong - everything that occurs to you. If you're really sorry, and you mean it, God will forgive you, because Jesus has died for all the ways you've messed up. You just need to tell God that you want to accept his gift of forgiveness and that you want to live with him and Jesus. Well, then you become a child of God. God actually adopts you! You can speak to him just like that. He's here now. People call it praying. Some people shut their eyes when they pray just to be able to concentrate better, and sometimes they clasp their hands,' Martin explained.

'Can you pray in twos?' Rebekka remembered that at the end of the YPM several people had prayed one after the other. Fortunately, someone had said a final 'Amen' before she'd felt that she had to pray something as well.

'Of course you can pray with other people. But why are you asking me all this?' Martin wanted to know.

Rebekka hesitated. Should she really risk it and become a Christian - right now? Eventually, the burning desire that she felt to have this loving God as her Father and Jesus as her Friend overcame her fears.

'Martin, would you pray with me that God will adopt me?'

A huge smile lit up Martin's face. He was beaming even more than he'd done at his birthday party.

'Of course, Bekki! You've no idea how happy your decision makes me feel. Come on, let's talk to God now. I'll pray first, and then you can pray. Is that okay?'

Rebekka nodded. Martin clasped his hands and closed his eyes and she did the same.

'God, you see us both here now,' Martin began, 'You've heard that Rebekka wants to be your child and I think it's really brilliant. I know that you're just as happy or even happier about it than I am. Thank you that your Son Jesus has died for all the things Rebekka has done wrong. Well, now she wants to say something to you herself.'

Rebekka hesitated a little. It was a bit strange simply speaking out loud into the room and believing that God heard it.

'God, I... em ... I'd like to have you as my Father like it was in the story on Friday. You know that I've done quite a lot of bad stuff, stealing, lying, copying homework and things like that. And that I've had bad thoughts about the creeps, I mean the teachers, and about other people as well. Oh yes, and using Daniel's computer behind his back - I know that's not right. I know for sure that he doesn't like me doing that... I've definitely done other things too, but I can't think of them at the moment. I'm asking you to forgive me and to - adopt me as your child. Thank you that Jesus died for me and that he wants to be my friend. I really don't deserve it. Please forgive me for not wanting anything to do with you for so long. Well, that's all, I think. Thank you - em - Amen!'

Rebekka and Martin looked at each other.

'Do you think he heard me?' Rebekka asked.

'Of course he did,' Martin replied. 'He's promised to do that. Now you belong to him. Maybe you don't feel different. You won't change overnight, and it'll take time for you to be able to understand everything in the Bible. It's a slow process. Step by step. But you're a child of God now and God will take care of you as your Father. He's forgiven you for everything you've done wrong.'

'Somehow I feel a bit easier now, like a big weight's

been lifted off me. I feel really happy.'

It was obvious to see that Martin was delighted as well.

'Martin, what happens now?'

Martin thought for a moment. 'You should definitely speak to God a lot. You don't need to shut your eyes to do that. When you're walking to school you can talk to him in your thoughts. You'll need to read a bit of the Bible each day, to get to know him better. We learn from it about how we should live. I admit that reading it isn't always easy. So how about if we read the Bible together? How do you feel about that?'

Rebekka was all for it. She was glad that Martin was there for her. He'd obviously have to explain a lot more to her.

'I think it's important for you to have contact with other Christians, for instance the people in the YPM. Of course, if you want to, you can spend time with other Christian groups, but who you spend time with is a deciding factor in being a Christian. You can easily give up, if you go it alone, you know.'

'Of course I'll come to the YPM I like the people there,' Rebekka replied 'Maybe we'll be able to meet up with Ulrike and Carmen at school and read the Bible during break time.'

Martin suddenly looked serious and glanced out of the window.

'What's the matter? Have I said something wrong?'

Martin turned to face her again and said eventually, 'No. It's just, because . . . I'm not going back to school any more.'

'Why? There's no way you're behind with the work

because you're so good at it all. What do you mean, you're not going to go to school any more?' She stared at him blankly.

'Perhaps you haven't realised, but these last three months at school have been torture. All those long corridors between classrooms, carrying a heavy bag - it's all been a bit too much for me. And after the holidays we'll be in the upper school, and we'll be on the third floor. I'd find it impossible to constantly climb the stairs. That's why I can't go to school again until I've had the transplant operation.'

Rebekka sat there feeling awkward. Actually, it had stuck out a mile that something like that was going to happen, but she'd always dismissed thoughts like that. She didn't want to believe that Martin was as ill as that.

'And if you . . . I mean, you could try going to another school. There are other schools in this area,' she eventually said.

Martin shook his head. 'No, we've already checked out every possible school. There wasn't one I'd be able to cope with in my state of health.'

'And so . . . what are you going to do at home?'

Martin looked helpless. 'Nothing - just wait. Perhaps I'll do a bit of writing, painting and crafts and stuff. Just what I can still manage to cope with.'

Rebekka had a huge lump in her throat. It was true that recently, Martin hadn't been coping very well. He often needed about quarter of an hour to recover from moving between classrooms. She could really understand why he didn't want to go to school in these circumstances. But nevertheless it was really a shame. He was a fairly bright pupil and he would have had brilliant marks in his final exams.

'I'll come and visit you every day, I promise. I won't desert you!'

Martin looked grateful. 'You shouldn't waste all your free time with me. You shouldn't feel that you have to visit me. I'm not that ill. I can still go about on my moped.'

Rebekka pondered the situation. There must be some way that Martin could still go to school. She didn't want him to be sitting around at home in future, feeling down and bored. It was quite ironic that she, of all people, was thinking along those lines, because she'd always imagined that nothing could be more blissful than escaping from that stupid school. But maybe the real reason was that she knew she'd miss Martin being with her at school.

'You know what? You're always saying that we can ask God about anything. So let's just ask him to find a way for you to continue going to school. Maybe God will work it so that the school is renovated and gets a lift installed, or maybe he'll work it so that the pager will bleep, you'll get a transplant operation right away and will be well enough for the beginning of the new term.'

Rebekka suddenly felt full of optimism again. Yes, she would ask her new Father right away to deal with the whole thing. Hadn't Martin always mentioned that God would only give what was best for him? And he certainly wouldn't want Martin to have to give up his education, allowing his brain to vegetate.

Martin looked at Rebekka in astonishment. He apparently hadn't expected that kind of thing from her - or at least not yet. 'You mean, I should just pray that God works it out somehow? Perhaps he doesn't want me to go to school any longer.'

'That's a lame excuse! If he's got something better planned for you, he'll tell us - won't he?'

Martin looked thoughtful and then said, 'You're right. If you've got such trust in God already, I want to be like that too.'

'Okay, let's pray then! You first!'

They closed their eyes again, and Martin began, 'Father in Heaven, you've just heard what Rebekka's said about the situation with school. I really don't know how I'm going to carry on. You know that I can't walk the long distances any more and how weak it's made me. But you've probably got a good idea about how I can go on. Please tell me what I should do. And if it's possible, may I be able to go to school again. I would really like to be able to take my final exams. But if you have something different planned, then that's okay too. You know what you're doing. I'm relying on you, as I always do, God. Amen.'

Rebekka prayed again too, 'God . . . em . . . Father, you surely know how good Martin is at his schoolwork. It would really be a pity if he didn't make the most of it, wouldn't it? Please do something so that Martin can sit his final exams. You can do it. Amen.' Rebekka was amazed herself at how much she trusted God. Somehow she felt that he was near and would make everything turn out for the best. Just like Martin had always told her.

THE SKETCHES

Rebekka was feeling a bit disappointed. Two weeks had gone by and there was no sign of a solution to Martin's difficulties. School would start again in three days' time and it would be even less enjoyable without Martin there. Perhaps God hadn't heard their prayers. She was almost a little annoyed at him. She didn't have any alternative apart from leaving , and yet she didn't want to do that either. She had to continue going whether she liked it or not.

Rebekka and Martin were sitting in her room once again.

'Rebekka!' Her mother shouted. Mum only called her 'Rebekka' when she was going to ask her to do something unpleasant.

'You haven't forgotten Gran's birthday, have you? What are you going to wear on Saturday?'

So that was Mum's game! Rebekka pulled a face. 'Oh no, the stupid birthday. Do I really have to go along?' She asked irritably.

'It's Gran's 75th! You'll surely be able to spare a few hours of your precious time for her. Or does Madam have something vitally important planned for Saturday? - probably consuming so many jelly bears that she won't even get into her newest pair of jeans?'

'Just leave me alone!' Rebekka yelled and slammed the door shut. To be on the safe side, she locked the door, so that Mum couldn't come in and annoy her any more.

Rebekka couldn't stand it when her mother spoke to her in that tone of voice.

'What have you got against this birthday?' Martin wanted to know. He was sitting on Rebekka's couch, looking baffled.

'That stupid woman really gets on my nerves - my Gran, I mean. She's got faith too, you know, but she's different from us. She's always floating around on cloud nine, and she always used to get on my nerves rabbeting on about some church service or other. Besides, it's her fault that I've got a name that everyone winds me up about.'

Martin looked at her with a serious expression on his face, and said eventually, 'I don't think that the way you speak about your Gran is right. Do you think God loves her one whit less than he loves you? Besides, he only forgives us when we forgive others. It says that in the Lord's prayer.'

Rebekka looked defiant. It was okay for Martin to talk - he didn't have her Gran. His was probably very nice and didn't treat him like a little kid. Even when Gran called her 'Little Bekki' or 'Bekki, pet', she felt like blowing her top. After all, she was fifteen now! Gran also poked her nose into things which weren't any of her business, like school for instance.

'It's alright for you to talk,' Rebekka countered. 'If I had your Gran, perhaps I'd be able to speak like that too, but mine is really annoying. Even though I'm a Christian, I can't stand her. I hate her!'

Martin wouldn't let up. 'And are you happy doing that?'

Rebekka didn't answer.

' I don't think you'll really be happy until you forgive your Gran. You can certainly ask God to help you to accept her.'

Rebekka could be just as stubborn as her friend.

'Do you always get on with everyone all the time then? Was there never even one person who you really didn't like?'

Martin said nothing at first and then said quietly, 'There was somebody. In the church in Bremen there was a pastor who was always criticising my best friend. It wasn't long before I got furious with this pastor. As if he didn't have any faults of his own! It got to the stage where in my eyes, everything he did was wrong. But I was desperately unhappy in the process myself, especially if he was at the YPM

Somehow, I knew deep down inside that I should forgive him, but it took quite a long time, until I forced myself to do that. It was only then that I felt better again. Later on, Herr Bergmahl (that was his name), told me that Andreas, my friend, has turned out to be one of his best church workers.'

Rebekka sat in her armchair, looking thoughtful. It was true that she didn't feel too great with all this loathing inside, but she didn't want to accept Gran just like that.

'Martin, you needed a long time before you were able

to forgive that man. Yet you expect me to forgive someone right away. Isn't that a bit unfair?'

Martin said nothing and then said at last, 'You're right. I can't expect you to do things immediately, when I needed a long time myself to do them. But please believe me that you'll feel a lot better when you forgive your Gran, and remind yourself instead that God loves her.'

After Martin had gone home, Rebekka considered what he'd said. If God would only forgive her if she forgave her Gran, things wouldn't go very well while she dug her heels in and refused.

'God,' she eventually prayed, 'You know that I don't like Gran. She really gets on my nerves. Martin said I should forgive her. It's easier said than done. God, I ask you to help me to accept Gran as she is. Help me to ignore it when she calls me 'Bekki pet' in future . . . I find it hard to believe that you love Gran as much as you love me, but Martin says you love everyone equally . . . that's probably in the Bible somewhere. God, I won't find it easy to stop being annoyed at Gran and to like her instead. But I want to forgive her. Honest. I'll prove it to you. I've already got an idea, God. Good night. Amen.'

Somehow Rebekka felt better. She even wanted to show God that she didn't feel mad at her Gran any more. She'd had an interesting idea. Gran's birthday celebrations were always dead boring, and she might be cheered up if someone (Martin, for instance) were to do something amusing in the middle of it. Rebekka knew that Gran always enjoyed watching comedy on TV.

She could perhaps even rehearse something with Martin beforehand. He'd certainly agree to it. He'd just have to - after all, he'd been the one who'd wanted her to forgive Gran. Rebekka felt genuinely excited when she visualised Gran's surprised face. The old lady only knew her as a sullen and permanently bad-tempered teenager. The last occasion she'd probably seen Rebekka laughing was on her twelfth birthday, when Gran had dropped a piece of cake onto the new dress she'd been showing off a couple of minutes earlier.

First thing the next morning Rebekka phoned Martin. 'Hi there, old chap, come on over. I've something important to tell you.'

'What about?' Martin wanted to know.

'I'm not going to tell you yet. But you'll definitely like it. See you then, bye.' She hung up. This method of doing things was nice and straightforward because she didn't have to listen to any possible objections, and Martin had no alternative but to come round. At any rate, it had always worked up until now.

A little while later, Martin was standing at the Jansens' front door.

'It's great that you've come over so soon. Let's go to my room,' Rebekka said when she saw him. They sat down on the sofa and Rebekka brought out a bag of jelly bears, which she'd acquired honestly, of course. The shop assistant had stared at her when she'd put ten bags down on the counter, and had asked, 'Are you a professional sweet-taster, or are you on a jelly bear diet?' She'd been spared such embarrassing questions when she'd pinched the things. But nevertheless she really did have an easier conscience now.

'First of all, I wanted to tell you that I thought about our conversation about my Gran for a long time, yesterday,' she began, 'and at last I've . . . forgiven her.'

Martin beamed at her. 'That's fantastic, Bekki! Do you feel better now?'

She nodded.

'I've had a cool brainwave too. That's why I phoned you. You see, I want to ask you to do me a favour.'

He looked at her with a puzzled expression on his face. What kind of scheme was she hatching up now?

'Well,' she explained, 'You're really good at acting out sketches. So I thought that Gran would really enjoy seeing you perform one or two at her birthday do.'

Martin didn't seem exactly enthusiastic.

'You want me to act in front of your Gran?'

'You don't have to, but you can if you want to!' Rebekka corrected him. 'Isn't it a great honour for you to be allowed to give of your best for my dear grandmother?' She asked, grinning mischievously. 'You wanted me to forgive my Gran and to accept her. Now you to have to take the consequences!'

What could Martin say to that? He admitted he was beaten.

'Well, okay, if you're sure your Gran will like it.'

'Maybe we could even act out a sketch together. I can usually learn things by heart quite fast. Have you got your sketches written down somewhere?'

Martin nodded. 'I think that's a better idea. I'd feel a bit stupid if I had to do a sketch by myself in front of complete strangers. But if you're acting too, then it's different.'

He nipped back home (if you could describe it as nipping in his case!) and returned again completely out of breath, looking blue and carrying a large book.

After he'd recovered a bit, he said, 'There are heaps

of sketches in here. Some of the ones about married couples are quite funny - we could both have a go at them.'

For the next hour they decided which would be the best sketches to perform. Martin didn't mind which ones they chose, because he knew almost all of them off by heart anyway. They eventually decided that they would act out two sketches together and then Martin would do a longer one by himself. Rebekka enjoyed practising them so much, that she wondered why she'd not done stuff like that before. There was a drama group at school which was taken by one of the more likeable teachers. Unfortunately, it wasn't Herr Becker, or Rebekka would have signed up for it ages ago.

They spent the next few afternoons rehearsing. Rebekka had actually succeeded in learning the two sketches in just one day. But . . . there were problems. Martin got so out of breath, after just five minutes, that he'd fall exhausted into the armchair to have a breather. There was no way he'd be able to put on his solo performance.

'It's a real shame, Martin! Gran would have enjoyed it so much.' It was a whole new feeling, wanting to make Gran happy. 'But with the best will in the world, it's not going to work.' Rebekka felt like howling her eyes out. She'd made such an effort to learn the sketches and to practice her roles, and now her great plan looked like it was going to fall through.

Martin said nothing for ages, then, 'We'll have a go, Bekki, but not on our own. God will help us if our motives are right. That's often happened to me. At home I've not been able to do things, but when I've left everything in God's hands it's turned out okay. I think it's because God wants me to rely on him and not on myself any more.'

Rebekka looked at him sceptically. God didn't seem to have helped Martin to go to school, why should he help out with the sketches?

'I don't know. Aren't you making it too simple, putting everything on to God? What'll we do if it all goes wrong?'

Martin seemed to be full of confidence again.

'I really believe that what we want to do is okay, and so God won't let us down. And I don't think it's all over as far as school is concerned, either.'

Was Martin able to read her thoughts? It almost seemed like it.

'Okay then, if you're really convinced that God won't say no, we should speak to him about it now.' They asked God to help them and to give Martin the breath he needed.

On Saturday Rebekka was excited and nervous. They hadn't even been able to completely rehearse everything because Martin had started to wheeze after only a short time. Now they were both sitting at one end of a long table covered with a feast of good food, in the restaurant where Gran was celebrating her birthday. Rebekka had asked her Gran if she could invite her friend, Martin, because he was a nice boy and she wouldn't find it so boring if he was there. She didn't want to give the surprise away.

They had finished their lunch. An atmosphere of boredom was beginning to descend. For some inexplicable reason, Gran usually invited people who were either so quiet, you'd have thought they'd taken a lifelong vow of silence, or else people who couldn't stand the sight of each other. Rebekka cautiously tapped her glass to attract attention. Her heart was beating so hard that she thought it would burst. Everyone stared at her as she began,

'Dear Gran,' (Gran hadn't been called that for at least eight years). 'Martin and I have planned a small surprise for you, to liven up the place . . . We're going to act out a sketch about a married couple for you.'

Martin and Rebekka went over to a table which had been set out beforehand and began. They did one sketch and Martin didn't wheeze once. They were only interrupted occasionally by laughter or applause.

When they'd finished, Rebekka noticed that Gran was moved to tears.

'That was wonderful! I don't know what to say!'

'We've got some more up our sleeves!' Rebekka replied. After the initial success, she'd regained her self-confidence. Gran didn't know what had hit her and seemed to be beside herself with happiness. Rebekka heard her whispering to Mum, 'And I always used to think that the child didn't like me. I was wrong to have thought that.' Rebekka had to hide a grin. If only Gran knew . . .

The second sketch went down really well. Rebekka and Martin gave each other a knowing look. They'd relied on God and he'd really helped them. But the highlight - Martin's solo sketch - was yet to come.

After a short break Martin went forward and started the sketch. Rebekka sent God one arrow prayer after another in her thoughts. Martin's solo performance went so well that people wanted an encore and Martin acted out another two sketches. When he sat down again, he hadn't turned blue and he wasn't out of breath either. In fact the opposite was the case - he hadn't looked so well in ages.

'Sometimes it blows my mind the way you do things, Lord. I'm sorry that I didn't believe you could do that. That was really a cool surprise .' Rebekka thought.

This was the only one of Gran's birthday do's which Rebekka had enjoyed. And she wasn't alone in that.

THE TROLLEY

School had started again, and Rebekka was missing Martin. But there had been one good new development - they'd escape from Herr Mertens for the next four weeks. He was lying in hospital because he'd broken his leg in several places. Herr Jürgens and others would stand in for him most of the time but there would sometimes be free periods.

Unfortunately, there was another piece of news which was the worst personal trauma that Rebekka had experienced in her entire school career. The best teacher of all time, Herr Becker, had decided to move to another school in six months' time. Rebekka couldn't imagine anything worse happening to her. Now there was virtually nothing that made school bearable apart from break times and the holidays of course. Life was tough. There was no way Martin could comprehend why she was so upset about this. He only said, 'Well, Bekki, there are still other good teachers around. Perhaps you'll really like the new one. And if you're not getting to grips with your English, then I can help you, or perhaps someone else.'

Sometimes Martin didn't understand at all. What had

English lessons to do with the man of her dreams, except that he happened to teach them? It was guaranteed that she'd never get another teacher like him.

Rebekka tried to keep Martin in the picture about what was going on at school as much as possible. She went over to visit him almost every day. Today she headed over to the Baumanns' house right after lunch. Sven let her in and she ran straight into Martin's room as usual, 'Hi, Martin, what are you . . .?' She stopped in mid-sentence. It was only now that she noticed that Martin was sitting in a wheelchair.

'What's that?' She asked, flabbergasted.

Martin grinned, 'Have you never seen a wheelchair before? Don't you think my new 'trolley' looks cool?'

Admittedly, he looked a whole lot better in his modern, dark red model, than he would have in one of the wheelchairs Rebekka had seen at the old people's home where her other Gran lived. But nevertheless, she was a bit shocked to see Martin sitting in a wheelchair.

'Is that your own personal one, then?' Rebekka asked after she'd got more used to the sight.

'Of course! It's cool, isn't it?'

'I don't know... What do you need a wheelchair for?'

'So I don't have to sit around at home. Now I can join in at last when the others from the YPM go for walks, drive to the park, or visit someone in hospital. Now we can go into town at last, Bekki, or go for a walk in the evenings . . . Look at what I can do!' Martin reversed a little, stopped jerkily and leaned back until the wheelchair was balancing only on the back wheels. Then he went slowly forward on just two wheels. Rebekka was not exactly enthusiastic.

'Cut it out! You'll fall over backwards! Perhaps you're right, it's maybe a good thing for you to have.'

For the next ten minutes Martin demonstrated what he could do with a "trolley" - taking off the arm- and footrests, folding it up and so on.

After they'd thoroughly investigated it all and tested it out, Martin asked, to change the subject, 'What's going on at school? Anything new?'

'No,' Rebekka replied. 'It's still standing! We had a free period today because Mertens is still in hospital .'

'Hey, I've an idea. How about going to visit him in hospital? My mother was planning to do some shopping in town later on in any case, and she'll be able to take us in. We can test drive my new trolley at the same time!'

Rebekka stared at him, stunned.

'You're not serious! You don't want to visit that jerk!'

'I'll admit he wasn't exactly my favourite teacher, but he won't have many visitors because he's so unpopular, and he doesn't have a family.'

'No wonder! No woman could stand more than a week with such a grouchy toad. Besides, he's got a father complex. He always calls everyone "my child."'

'Bekki, there might be reasons why he's become like that. Don't run him down so much,' Martin tried to calm her down.

'Okay, I take back what I said about him being a grouchy toad, but do you really want to visit that guy?'

'Of course. I'm sure he'll be pleased to have visitors. I'm dying for a chance to test drive my trolley properly at last. I'm limited in how I can use it here in my room. Come on, Bekki, make an effort and say you'll come!'

He looked at her with such a pleading expression that

she eventually agreed to go.

'Okay, but just for a short time. You won't have to bump into him again but I'll soon have to see him every day in school again. If he mentioned in front of other people that I'd visited him, I'd be dead embarrassed. But I won't win an argument with you, so let's go. You do have some dumb ideas sometimes.'

'Bekki, I'm sure it'll be fun. Just wait and see.'

Frau Baumann was willing to give them a lift to the hospital and to pick them up again about half an hour later. Sven helped to put the wheelchair quickly into the car. That was what was so different from Rebekka's family. Here everyone pulled together and everyone was there for each other when they needed help. When she needed someone, no one had the time, let alone the interest. She often wished she belonged to Martin's family instead of her own. It was almost the case anyway, because of the large amount of time she spent over there.

Once they arrived at the hospital they found out which ward Herr Mertens was in. They had quite a long way to walk, or in Martin's case to wheel.

'Let me wheel myself,' Martin said. 'It'll be good fun on this smooth surface.'

Rebekka let him go and he went tearing off.

'Hey, wait for me!' she yelled after him. What a guy!

But Martin didn't get very far. After about twenty metres he stopped because he was gasping for breath. Rebekka came running up to him.

'You're really off your head sometimes! Now you look totally shattered again! What was the point of doing that?'

'But it was fun,' Martin replied.

Rebekka just shook her head and pushed him slowly towards the mens' surgical ward.

Apprehensively, they knocked at the door of the hospital room. The beating of their hearts seemed even louder.

'Come in,' someone shouted from inside. They both walked in. Martin left the wheelchair outside, because it would have probably been too awkward to manoeuvre inside the room. He could still walk in any case.

'Who's there? What a surprise! You're visiting *me?*' Herr Mertens shouted. He was lying on his bed, with a huge plastercast on his leg. There were piles of Mickey Mouse and Donald Duck comics lying on the duvet. Who would have imagined he read stuff like that?

'Hello, Herr Mertens. How are you?' Martin spoke first.

'As well as one would expect under the circumstances. I didn't expect to see you coming to visit me. How are things at school without me?'

Rebekka almost came out with the comment, 'Much better!' but she managed to control herself in time. 'Quite well, actually,' she said instead.

'And Martin will still be a whizz-kid at biology (the best of all subjects), I presume?' Herr Mertens asked.

'I'm not at school any more,' Martin explained.

His ex-teacher stared at him in astonishment. 'I'd never have thought that you of all people would have gone in for an apprenticeship. You would have passed your final exams with flying colours, my child!'

'You misunderstood me. Walking the long corridors at school is too exhausting, so for now I'm not going to school until I hopefully get the transplant operation.'

Herr Mertens looked at him, full of consternation. 'That really is a pity. But actually it's not legal. School attendance is compulsory for twelve years. You can't stop going, just like that.'

Martin and Rebekka looked at each other in amazement. Up until then, they'd assumed that school attendance was only compulsory for ten years.

'Are you sure? Isn't it just ten years?' Martin asked. Herr Mertens shook his head.

'I'm one hundred percent certain that it's twelve years. So the state is still responsible for you, child. I wonder what we can do about it . . . It would be a crying shame if your intelligence was just to go to waste'

Martin stared at the floor in embarrassment. He didn't think of himself as being particularly intelligent.

'I've got an idea. It would probably be possible to arrange private tuition for you by some of the teachers at school. It would mean the teachers would come to your home and give you one-to-one tuition.'

'Just especially for me? They'd never do that just for me. I could never afford to pay them,' Martin objected.

Herr Mertens smiled, which was something he did only on rare occasions.

'You don't understand what I mean, child. The state would pay for the lessons. The teachers' tuition at your house would be calculated as part of their regular hours. I really think it would work.'

Rebekka stared at Martin, then at Herr Mertens, and then looked back at Martin again. Was this God's answer to their prayers?

'I think I'll get on to this right away. I've got plenty of time here in hospital and the telephone is sitting there not

115

being used. Besides, I've got a hot-line to the education department.'

'You'd do that for me? Private tuition doesn't sound too bad.' Martin seemed to be very taken with the idea.

Rebekka didn't know what to make of it. She 'd have preferred Martin to be back with her at school, but that was probably selfish. After spending about half an hour with Herr Mertens, they left. He'd apparently enjoyed their visit. He'd told them to come back in four days' time. Over that time he intended to get hold of every possible piece of information regarding private tuition.

'It'd be really brilliant if Mertens gets the private tuition off the ground and it goes ahead!' Martin was intrigued by the thought that he might soon be able to be educated within his own four walls.

'Perhaps it was a good thing that we visited Herr Mertens after all,' Rebekka commented.

While they waited at the hospital entrance for Frau Baumann, Martin said, 'By the way, I composed a song in honour of my trolley, this afternoon. Want to read it?'

'What a dumb question, of course I do.' Martin fished out a piece of crumpled paper from his pocket - typical of Martin! He handed it to Rebekka who read it at once.

My dearest trolley, whom I adore,
Each day I appreciate you more,
It's fun to drive you and to steer,
You are the best, to me it's clear
You're top of the range, you take me far,
So I dub you Baumann's Mega Wonder-car.
With these three words I now create
the letters BMW to abbreviate.

Refrain:
This is the BMW-rap.
When I'm cruising round the house, it takes a lot
of nerve,
As around Mum's furniture, I weave n' brake n
swerve.
When I see others struggling to walk and stride,
Then my BMW simply fills me with pride!

I used to think it would be jolly,
If I had just such a trolley,
Such a luxury is mega cool,
Don't need to walk or stand like a fool.
I've got comfort and style, it's just first-rate,
And it takes no sweat to accelerate!
And now it's hard to believe it's for real,
My dream's come true, I can free-wheel!

Once I had to stay alone here every day,
While others could walk and run further away,
Class trips and outings were out for me,
I missed out on quite a lot, you see.
But since I've got you trolley, I'm no longer sad,
The advantages you bring, make me feel glad.
I'm so happy, the dream's become reality,
And I thank God, who provided you for me.

'Sometimes, I wonder if you've a screw loose or else you're simply off your trolley!' Rebekka commented with a mischievous smile.

NEW PROSPECTS

Ever since Herr Mertens had put the idea of private tuition into their heads, Rebekka and Martin had talked about almost nothing else. Even Frau Baumann thought that the possibility was great, but she felt that it wasn't feasible in practice. Why should the teachers bother to make the effort to teach Martin by himself at their home? After all, he wasn't a boy-wonder with an extraordinarily high IQ., or the son of a king or president. He was only an average pupil from an ordinary family. Why should he be entitled to the luxury of private tuition?

Rebekka remembered how she'd prayed and asked God to provide a way for Martin to still be able to go to school.

'Do you think the private tuition thing could be an answer to our prayers?' She asked Martin.

'It's possible. It wouldn't be bad, but the thought of spending two hours being taught by guys like Mertens or Oswalt by myself, with no one to distract me, or to help me, is not exactly appealing.'

Oswalt was their French teacher who mumbled in such a monotone that towards the end of his lessons, even the most alert pupils were struggling not to fall asleep.

'The way I see it, I'm sure you'll get only nice teachers,' Rebekka tried to cheer him up.

She imagined how great it would be, if Herr Becker was her private tutor. That would be totally brilliant! If the home tuition worked out, she'd be quite envious of Martin, provided that he got the right teachers.

Tuesday came round at last. Today they'd find out what Herr Mertens had managed to wangle out of the education department. Martin could hardly bear the suspense. Why did Rebekka have to stay on at school so late, today of all days? But eventually, they could set off on their visit, and this time Frau Baumann came along too. She wanted to know the outcome of the private tuition as well.

When the three of them walked into the hospital room and said hello, they noticed that Herr Mertens was in a very good mood.

'I've been waiting for you. There's good news!' He announced. He was beaming as happily as he'd done when the marks of his pupils in the class test had improved to a higher average for the first time.

His visitors looked at him expectantly.

'Have you phoned the education department?' Martin asked. He couldn't contain his impatience any longer.

Herr Mertens nodded vigorously.

'First of all, I told the people there all about you and how talented you are. You've always worked so well in biology, child. Especially when we were studying the greenhouse effect. I remember you always summarised and described everything so accurately. The greenhouse effect is a very important topic, especially nowadays when

119

the hole in the ozone is growing. Aerosols should be produced without using poisonous substances. Personally, I am fundamentally against all perfumes, deodorants and all that paraphernalia. But if they have to produce the stuff then they should at least avoid using poisonous gases, don't you agree? Otherwise the problems caused by the greenhouse effect . . .'

Rebekka had to try hard not to scream. The greenhouse effect didn't interest her in the slightest at the moment. She could well understand why Herr Mertens didn't have a wife. She wished the guy would get to the point and tell them what he'd found out.

'You're certainly right there,' Martin interrupted, 'But at the moment I'm much more interested in what the education department said.'

'Oh yes, the education department. Well, I told them what a good pupil you are and how it would be a pity if you couldn't attend school any more.'

Was he going to start from the very beginning again? It just wasn't real!

'I mentioned the business about twelve years' compulsory school attendance too, child. And then I asked them whether there was such a thing available as private tuition. What concerns us though . . .'

How in the world did a guy like Herr Mertens ever manage to become a teacher when he repeated himself constantly before he ever got to the point? He really had a nerve to keep them in such an agony of suspense!

'At first they maintained that they had never done anything like that before and that they weren't aware of a similar case. But of course I didn't give up. Edelbert Mertens never gives up easily!'

So his name was Edelbert - poor bloke! The name was even worse than Rebekka!

'Then I asked if something like that was totally out of the question because you are still legally obliged to attend school. But the civil servant didn't know, so I asked to speak to his boss.'

Martin looked at him full of admiration. Somehow it was really nice of Herr Mertens to fight for his cause - in spite of the pranks Martin had played on him in the past.

'Well, I'll be brief.'

'At last!' Rebekka thought.

'Theoretically, the private tuition can go ahead. Mind you, we'll need to go through all the formalities.'

'What formalities?' Frau Baumann couldn't hide her surprise and happiness.

'First of all, Martin will have to register at a secondary school,' Herr Mertens explained with a self-important expression on his face. He seemed to be very conscious of how much he had achieved.

'Then they'll need a medical certificate to confirm that Martin is unable to attend a state school for health reasons. And then hopefully, teaching staff who can tutor Martin privately can be found. It goes without saying that the education authorities will finance it. There's likely to be a large amount of red tape but I think that overall we're going to succeed.' Herr Mertens leaned back in his bed, looked satisfied, as if his contribution to the successful outcome of the project had been completed.

'Thank you for all the trouble you've gone to. It was really very good of you,' Frau Baumann said.

'Oh, I enjoyed being of assistance.'

At this point a nurse entered the room. 'Herr Mertens,

we'll have to take you for another X-ray. Something went wrong the last time!' She informed the patient.

'That's okay, nurse. Thanks a lot! Yes, well, I'll have to say goodbye first. I hope that the tuition works out. It would be ridiculous if we didn't succeed after all this, wouldn't it? Keep me up to date with what's happening. I'll be very interested to hear!'

The three of them said goodbye and left the room.

Over the next few days the arrangements for private tuition were firing on all four cylinders. Almost every day when Rebekka went round to the Baumanns' house, there was more news. First of all, Martin had registered at school, and then they'd asked the university clinic for a medical certificate. They had to go through quite a lot of red tape but amazingly enough, all the civil servants involved had a favourable view of private tuition, even though it was the first time that they'd heard of such a thing. They all seemed to be curious to find out if the education department would authorise it. Even Martin's former doctor, who'd known him since he was small, left no stone unturned in order to speed up the process. Herr Mertens rang up the Baumanns to find out the latest news so often that it began to get on Martin's nerves.

At last they got there. The education department authorised it and now they needed to find teachers.

'Just imagine, Martin, there's a piece of paper hanging up in the staffroom which the teachers need to sign if they want to tutor you - four teachers are needed altogether.' Rebekka informed her friend. 'But you surely won't be able to cover all the subjects with only four teachers . . .' she wondered. 'Will you only be taught the main subjects from now on?'

Martin shook his head. 'No, I'm going to have three more teachers from another school because one can't spare so many.'

Rebekka thought for a moment.

'Wow, Martin, then maybe you'll get Herr Becker after all?'

'If I do, then I hope it's a Frau Becker, and that she's equally good looking!' Martin commented, giving her a wink.

Every day Rebekka had a look to see if more teachers had signed up. Eventually there were four names - Herr Kurz, Rebekka's art teacher, and three others - Frau Seemann, Herr Schmid, and Herr Jennings - Rebekka didn't know them. Herr Kurz was okay really. He had a sense of humour and it was easy to distract him from his topic. Rebekka was dying to find out who the other three would be.

Things didn't begin immediately. First of all, one teacher after another was invited for a cup of tea just so that they could spend time getting to know each other. Martin had never chatted to teachers in such a relaxed atmosphere before. He kindly arranged the timing of the visits so that Rebekka could be there as well. She was dying of curiosity.

'I think they're all okay,' she voiced her opinion, after the third teacher, Herr Jennings, had introduced himself.

'Somehow, they don't seem the same as the old teachers in school, when they're here. They're really laid back! Hey, you're going to have an easy time of it if they're like that when they're teaching you. I think you could even get to like them.'

'I've found them all nice too - up until now!' He added

with a meaningful look. 'The other four will probably be "nasty toads and battle-axes" to use your usual apt descriptions! By the way, I now know the names of the three teachers from the other school. But you'll be disappointed - Herr Becker's not among them. I haven't met any of them yet but they sounded nice on the phone. We'll just to have to wait and see.'

'Yes, let's see.'

I'M JUST A BURDEN
FOR EVERYONE

Rebekka sat on her chair, feeling restless and constantly glancing at the clock. Krom was still going on about the French Revolution in 1789 and this was the fifth history period they'd spent on it. It was slowly beginning to bug her. She couldn't care less about history.

'I wish someone would invent a machine which would speed up time when it was necessary,' she thought. Then she wouldn't have given the old bloke spouting in front of her the chance to utter even one more sentence about the French Revolution. Martin was having a cushy time - he'd got a dead nice history teacher. He also had no more than three hours of lessons each day. The private tuition had been going really well. Martin was content at any rate and there was a lot of camaraderie between him and most of his tutors. Sometimes the lessons were so funny that he had sore stomach muscles because he'd laughed so much. One teacher even brought along biscuits or chocolates or stuff like that. She wished that would happen at school! Frau Baumann made an effort too, and provided coffee and biscuits during the lessons. As far as education was concerned, Martin had a lot going for him.

At long last the break time bell rang. Freedom! Rebekka was just about to walk out into the playground when Kai barred her way.

'Well, baby - what's your Martian up to? The weakling doesn't dare to come to school any more? He's probably scared of me, isn't he?'

'You'd love that, wouldn't you?' Rebekka replied sarcastically and pushed past Kai.

He seemed to be missing Martin too. It was boring without him. Maren had left school after fourth year and had started training as a hairdresser. Ina was constantly head over heels in love with some guy or other. She got on everyone's nerves by going on about how great her new fella was, whether anyone wanted to hear about it or not. Apparently, they were going to move in together, although she'd never done that before, or they'd maybe even get married, although of course they'd both be very tolerant, whatever that was supposed to mean.

The only ray of hope was that Ulrike, a girl from the YPM, had moved into Rebekka's class. She helped with the little tots' group. Rebekka found it easy to chat with her, although she was a bit bossy, but she was nice.

'What do you actually do with the little hooligans at the little tots' club?' Rebekka wanted to know.

'Oh, all kinds of things - we play games, sing, tell Bible stories, do crafts, have parties - just the same sort of things that go on at any nursery. The only difference is that we want to share God's love with them,' Ulrike explained.

Rebekka was fond of little kids. She was sorry she didn't have any little brothers or sisters. She wondered if she could help at the little tots' club.

'Hey, could you do with another helper there?' She asked.

Ulrike smiled at her, 'Of course. Are you offering?'

Rebekka nodded. 'I've never done stuff like that before. Maybe, I wouldn't be any good at it,' she admitted.

'Rubbish,' Ulrike tried to dispel Rebekka's doubts. 'Believe me, you can soon pick up that kind of thing. The first few times you can just come along and watch, and that way the children can get to know you too.'

Rebekka agreed. That way, if she didn't like it, she could always drop out.

'When do you meet?'

'Monday at three.'

'Okay, I'll be there.'

It was a really lovely day. Just the sort of weather for a cycle run. But Rebekka had promised Martin she'd call in on him. Too bad! She wasn't really in the mood. She'd just phone and say she couldn't make it. She dialled the Baumanns' number.

'Martin Baumann speaking,' her friend answered at the other end of the line.

'Hi, Martin - it's Bekki. I just wanted to let you know that I'm not coming today after all.'

'Why not?' Martin wanted to know.

'Well, it's such a great day - I thought I'd go out on my bike for a while,'

'We could go for a walk with my trolley.'

'Oh, I don't really feel like it. You don't get the breeze blowing through your hair that way. Besides, I was round at yours' yesterday I'd like to spend some time by myself.'

'I get it. I'm just a nuisance to you. It's not exactly appealing to push a moron like me round the village ... go and take a ride on your fab bike!'

Click ... He'd hung up! What had suddenly got into him? He didn't own her! So what, she wasn't going to feel guilty about it and let it spoil her bike ride. If he was acting so stupidly today, she didn't want to visit him anyway.

Rebekka did a couple of laps on her mountain bike but she wasn't really enjoying it. She kept thinking about Martin. Why was he behaving in such a weird way today? Over the past few months she'd noticed that there had been occasions when Martin had been easily offended or bad tempered. He wasn't very good at handling criticism, at least, not initially. If she'd pointed out something that he'd done wrong, he would immediately start to defend and justify himself, instead of recognising his mistake. He could get really worked up. But after a few hours he would usually apologise and admit he'd perhaps messed up a bit. But today his voice had sounded somehow sad and frustrated. Rebekka couldn't stop thinking about it - she had to find out what was wrong. Besides she wanted to read a bit in the Bible with Martin as well. She rang the Baumanns' bell and Martin opened the door.

'Hi,' Rebekka said.

'Hello,' Martin said in a depressed tone of voice, and went back into his room again, as if he didn't want anything to do with Rebekka.

But Rebekka didn't give up so easily. She ran after him, and barred his way in the doorway.

'Hey, can you at least tell me what's up with you?'

'Nothing,' Martin snarled, not even looking at her. 'Go off on your bike again! You don't need to waste your precious time on me.'

'Are you having me on? You're talking rubbish. You know full well that I like coming here. If you're grumpy because I didn't want to come just one single time - that's unfair and mean of you! I've got the right to spend some time on my own. After all, I'm not your sole entertainer!'

What had got into him? Martin couldn't expect her to spend every moment of her time with him.

'I said you shouldn't fritter away your time seeing me!'

Martin turned away and Rebekka realised that he was struggling to hold back tears.

'I know I'm just a nuisance to everyone. You'd all be glad if I was dead!' He added quietly - 'Kai was totally right. Someone like me shouldn't be a burden to society. I'm no use to anyone. I only cost money and energy and I get on people's nerves.'

Rebekka was horrified. She'd never heard Martin speaking like that before. He was usually cheerful and he loved life. What was wrong with him? How could he imagine that anyone could wish him dead?

'Stop speaking such trash! You know that we're all very fond of you. What other family would support you the way yours does?' She pointed out.

'But I can never make it up to them. I'm just taking from everyone all the time. My family do everything for me, the teachers have to come to the house especially for me, and you're always visiting. But I - I'm no use to anyone! What Kai used to say was right - I'm the scum of the earth!'

Then Martin began to cry. Rebekka felt helpless. If only some of the Baumanns were at home! But Frau Baumann and Sven were in town, they'd mentioned they were going there, yesterday, and Herr Baumann was still at work.

'Martin,' she said eventually, 'Please stop. There's no one I care about as much as you,' (Apart from Herr Becker, she thought). 'I'd be devastated if you died. You know that. What would I do without you? Who would help me with my maths and biology and who'd read the Bible with me? You're the only one I can talk to about everything.'

Martin said nothing. A few tears ran down his cheek. By now, Rebekka felt like crying too.

'It's good that you're around, Bekki,' Martin said after a while.

Rebekka gave Martin a hug and said nothing. That seemed to do him good. They remained sitting like that for a while.

'Martin, I'd like to help with the little tots' group. Do you think I can do it?' Rebekka eventually asked.

'Definitely,' Martin replied and smiled at her.

It wasn't the last time that Martin felt so frustrated. Over and over again he'd say that Kai had been right and that he was useless. Rebekka realised that Martin had not been as unaffected by Kai's constant insults as she'd thought. With time, she realised too that it helped Martin most when she didn't say much, but just occasionally gave him a hug and listened until he'd got everything off his chest. It didn't help at all if she told him not to be so ungrateful or if his mother warned him not to sin against God by wishing he was dead.

'I'm glad that we're friends,' Rebekka thought. 'And that Martin isn't always in control of things. He can understand me then, when I'm sometimes down. I think it's good that he needs me too.'

MARTIN'S FUNERAL

Today, for the first time, Rebekka had planned and led the games at the little tots' club. They'd all had a whale of a time. The kids had got to know her really well. She'd been there eight weeks now. She was really taken with four year old Pascal. He was a really comical little boy. She'd even forgiven him for the fact that he'd trodden on her hand three times when they were playing "Ring'A'Roses" which wasn't exactly a delightful experience because he was fairly plump. If someone had told her a year ago that she'd be playing "Ring'A'Roses" and "Who's the King of the Castle?" with little kids, she'd have laughed.

'Bekki, do you know why I like you so much?' Pascal asked her.

Rebekka shook her head.

'Because you're fat and cuddly. I love you to bits!'

Rebekka laughed. When did she ever get a compliment like that?

She was sad every time the tots' group was over. At the end of each session, Carmen, Ulrike and Rebekka would prepare for the following week.

'You did a great job leading those games! I think the kids have really taken to you!' Carmen patted her approvingly on the shoulder.

Rebekka liked Carmen almost more than Ulrike, but she got on very well with both of them.

'Do you want to have a go at telling the story next time?' Ulrike asked.

'I don't know. I've never done that before. Which one is it?'

'The story of the lost son. Do you know it?'

Rebekka nodded. There was no other story she remembered as well as that one. It had persuaded her to turn to God.

'Okay, I think it's a great story, after all!'

Over the past four months Rebekka had been to the YPM and to church several times. The services were similar to ones she'd been to before, and yet different. Usually, they began with singing and everyone would join in heartily. Or else the choir would sing, not as cool as hard rock maybe, but quite nice in a different sort of way. Sometimes Markus interviewed one of the members of the church so that people got to know each other better. It was usually very interesting. Some people had really experienced tough times, and yet they were incredibly cheerful. Before the sermon, which was usually long, and which Rebekka sometimes couldn't completely understand, there would be notices about what would be happening during the next week. Rebekka felt incredibly proud, when the pastor had announced, 'On Monday there's the little tots' club. Rebekka Jansen is now helping with it and we're really pleased about that. We wish you a lot of fun with the little ones, Rebekka!'

Martin had smiled at her approvingly, looking pleased. He seemed to be equally glad that she felt so much at home in the church. The Sunday morning before, she'd even called round for her Gran on the way to the service. When she'd asked 'Morning, Gran. Do you want to come to church with me?' The elderly lady had looked at her, as flabbergasted as if Rebekka had asked if she wanted to marry Herr Mertens! At the end of the service, she'd suggested an idea to pastor Klinkel and he had been really enthusiastic about it. She wanted to design a programme, with Martin's help, for the church service and then hand them out in church on Sundays. This would mean that people who were coming to church for the first time, for example those attending confirmation classes, would find it easier to follow what was going on.

The little tots' group usually finished at around five, and that included their time of discussion afterwards. Rebekka had enough time to go round to Martin's before the thriller was due to start on TV. She hadn't bothered with supper for the past three days because she'd decided to lose a bit of weight, even if it meant risking not being as cuddly as Aunty Editaud any more. The decisive factor had been that she now had only one pair of trousers that still fitted. It was true that she could have bought some new clothes, but the larger sizes were always more expensive . . .

Martin was in the middle of writing an English essay when Rebekka arrived.

'Well, how was the large-scale operation at the tots' group today?' He asked.

'Good. No fatalities - only two casualties - a scratch on Elisabeth's right hand and a bump on Kevin's head,'

Rebekka reported.

Martin laughed, 'It sounds very dangerous. What do you do to the poor children?'

He packed his school work away and got out a game which they'd started the day before.

'Do you want to carry on with the game?' He asked.

Of course she wanted to! It was really weird that she now really enjoyed doing things like that when they would have bored her stiff a year ago.

'Oh, did I tell you that Frau Schumann has died?' Rebekka said after they'd got themselves settled.

'Frau Schumann?' Martin looked shocked.

'Yes, Herr Jürgens told us this morning. Her car crashed into a lorry yesterday and she was killed instantly. He didn't really know how it had happened. The funeral is on Friday. There will be a short memorial service for her at the school too.'

Martin stared awkwardly at the floor.

'Man, how quickly it can happen. It's just as well she wasn't married and didn't have children. It would have been even worse then . . . I'm sorry it's happened. As a human being Schumann was alright, even if she wasn't the most brilliant of teachers. She must have only been in her forties . . . Are you going to the funeral?'

Rebekka shrugged her shoulders.

'I don't know yet. I don't particularly like funerals. They're always terribly sad. When the relatives cry, I always feel helpless and awkward and out of place.'

Martin said suddenly 'I don't want my funeral to be sad.'

Rebekka looked at him in astonishment, 'Don't talk rot! You're not going to die - and that's that!'

But Martin wouldn't get off the subject.

'I've imagined the way it should be if I don't get a transplant operation or don't survive it. I want my funeral to be a celebration! There should be a buffet laid on and our choir should sing cheerful songs.'

Rebekka stared at him, dumbfounded.

'Are you totally callous?'

Martin shook his head, 'I've really thought about it. The people who can't stand me, like Kai, for instance, will be really happy because they'll be rid of me at last. And the ones who like me should be glad because I'll be with God, and I'll be totally well there!'

Rebekka didn't know what to say. She thought it was somehow wrong and even morbid to discuss someone's funeral with them when they were still alive, although you obviously couldn't when they weren't. Besides, she found Martin's picture of his funeral downright unrealistic. You couldn't expect people who are mourning to be happy! It wasn't as simple as that. It was true that Martin would be with God when he died, Rebekka was certain of that. But in spite of that, his family and friends would be terribly sad that he'd no longer be there with them. She found the idea of celebrating his death with a buffet gruesome.

'Have you told all this to your mother?' She asked after a while.

'Of course,' Martin answered.

'And what does she think about it?'

'Oh, she wasn't very enthusiastic. She doesn't understand what I mean. I just don't want anyone to be sad when I'm with God and everything's great for me. If I'm happy with God, surely others should be able to feel the same too. Is that really too hard to understand?'

He looked at Rebekka.

When she seriously thought about it, she could follow his way of thinking. If you looked at the whole thing from his perspective, there would really be no reason to be sad. But presumably his wish couldn't be fulfilled in reality. There'd be a huge scandal about it and people wouldn't understand why this funeral was so different.

'I think I'd get really upset if I went along to Frau Schumann's funeral, for instance, not knowing what it'd be like, and I was confronted with a buffet and happy sounding music. People probably wouldn't be able to face that at your funeral either, even if you want it, yourself, Martin!'

Martin shrugged his shoulders.

'You're probably right. Nevertheless, I'd find that much nicer and more appropriate.'

For the next few minutes or so, they continued playing their game in silence, each deep in their own thoughts. Even if Martin's funeral would definitely never take the form he wished for, it was good to know that he would be with God, his heavenly Father, where he'd be really well and happy at last. Somehow this thought comforted Rebekka and took away a lot of her fear about Martin dying.

MARTIN IS NO ANGEL

It was a hot day. Rebekka was pushing Martin in his 'trolley' in the pedestrian precinct in town. Now and again, they'd pause and look into shop windows. They stopped outside an Oxfam shop for ages, because Martin couldn't take his eyes off a wonderful set of South American panpipes. They were priced at forty Marks. A lot of money, especially if you were nearly broke . . .

'Man, I'd really like to have them,' he sighed. Rebekka secretly counted her money as he gazed admiringly at the panpipes. She had just over 60 Marks with her.

'You know what, I'll buy them for you,' she decided.

Martin protested, 'No, I don't want you to do that. You shouldn't spend your money on me. You're doing me enough of a favour by wheeling me around town.'

'Rubbish. In the first place, I get more pocket money than you, and in the second , you got me out of hot water that time they caught me pinching stuff, and thirdly, it's about time I treated you to something. Come on, let's buy the thing!'

When Rebekka adopted this tone of voice, it was fairly pointless arguing with her. Martin had come to realise that over the time he'd known her. But this time he didn't object. As the wheelchair was too wide to go through the shop doorway, Martin decided to leave it outside. So he stood up and walked a few steps . . . and then he nearly had to sit down again with shock. A man who had been watching them from a few metres away, suddenly shouted, 'It's a miracle! A miracle's happened! He can walk again! It's a miracle!'

Everyone turned round and stared at the two of them and Rebekka turned as red as beetroot, which added even more to her embarrassment.

'No!' Martin explained, trying to drown out the man's words, 'It's not a miracle! I can still walk, but only short distances, because I've got heart disease. That's why I have the wheelchair.'

Slowly the excitement died down. People walked away, including the man who seemed to be disappointed. Martin and Rebekka were glad to get inside the shop and buy the panpipes. Martin played a few notes on them straight away, much to the shop assistant's delight.

'We sell a lot of these pipes, but this is the first time I've heard someone playing them,' she said smiling.

Martin was over the moon with his new acquisition and when there weren't so many people around, he'd play them, as Rebekka pushed him along in the wheelchair.

'These pipes have a much softer, more beautiful sound than mine at home, because they're made of very fine bamboo,' he said enthusiastically.

Rebekka came to an abrupt halt.

'What's wrong?' Martin asked.

'Look!' She whispered, 'Herr Becker's over there!'

'Where?'

'Over there! Come on, let's go and say hello to him!'

Martin groaned. Why did girls always have to fall for their teachers?

'Hello, Herr Becker!' Rebekka shouted from a distance.

'Oh, hello! What are you two doing here?' Herr Becker greeted them.

'We're having a stroll through town. Can we invite you to have an ice-cream with us?' Martin asked, and Rebekka felt so embarrassed, she wished the earth would swallow her up. Martin was going a bit over the top, inviting him to have an ice-cream with them!

'Thanks, I could do with an ice-cream in this heat. There's quite a nice cafe over there.'

After they'd ordered, Herr Becker turned to Martin and said, 'So, you're getting private tuition at home now?'

Martin nodded.

'I think that's fantastic. I'd never heard of that being done before, so I was surprised when Rebekka told me about it. That's really great. What are your tutors like? Are they all as terrible as those of us at school?'

'No, mine are naturally much, much nicer!' Martin said, grinning.

'Well, everything's cushy then!' Herr Becker laughed. He had a good sense of humour.

'Thanks for the super poems, by the way. You've got a real talent there!'

Rebekka signalled to Herr Becker to keep quiet, which he picked up on immediately.

'What poems?'

'Oh, Rebekka said you were good at writing poetry. Are you getting private lessons in every subject then?'

He quickly changed the subject.

Martin gave Rebekka a sharp glare. He appeared to have noticed that something was up. What a pain! If only Herr Becker hadn't mentioned the poems! But Martin was too polite to make a scene about it, and so he replied to Herr Becker's question as if he hadn't noticed anything.

'I've got English, French, Social Science, Biology, Art, German, Religious Studies, Maths and History. There weren't enough teachers for more subjects, but all of the main ones are covered.'

'That's really excellent! And what are you up to, Rebekka? Are you still so fluent in English?'

Rebekka blushed slightly. So he had noticed that she'd made an effort. She felt so flustered that she didn't know what to say. At the same time, she couldn't have wished for anything better than being able to chat privately with her beloved ex-teacher. But now she was so nervous, it wasn't as romantic and casual as she'd dreamed it would be.

'The new teacher is not so cool . . em . . . good. I mean, he's not so good at explaining things . . . em . . . he speaks in such a boring way . . .' she eventually stammered. Why did she have to be so shy and always at the most inconvenient times! But Herr Becker seemed to overlook her shyness.

'If you're struggling with your English, I'm sure Martin would help you, won't he?'

Rebekka nodded.

'No,' Martin disagreed. 'Bekki can manage by herself.'

Meanwhile the waiter had brought the ice-cream. It

was really delicious! Hopefully Martin would forget about what had been said about the poems earlier.

After Herr Becker had eaten his ice-cream, he said, after a glance at his watch, 'Is that the time? I should be home by now! Unfortunately, I'll have to leave you, folks. It was nice talking to you. All the best to you both, especially to you, Martin, with your personal tuition and your big operation. I'm sure you'll cope, knowing you! Bye!'

He went to the cash desk, and paid for the ice-creams. He was a great guy - and very nice!

It was time to think about heading home too. Sven had been visiting his friend, Simon, and he had arranged to pick them up at five. On the way, Martin didn't say a word. Rebekka was silent as well. She had a dark premonition that there was going to be huge explosion.

It was only when they were in Martin's room that he broke the silence,

'Come on, tell me what Herr Becker meant about the poems!'

'He didn't mean anything. Just forget it, okay?' Rebekka tried to get herself out of it. But she wasn't going to get away with it as easily as that.

'Don't lie, Bekki! You've been up to something!' His tone was sharp. Rebekka didn't want to look him in the eye. How could she explain it all to him?

'Once when you were away at the university clinic,' she began at last in almost a whisper, 'I asked Sven to print out your poems for me. I knew that you had them on the computer.'

'And he agreed just like that?'

'I said that you'd given your permission and that I

needed them urgently.'

'And then what?' Martin snapped.

Rebekka desperately tried to find the right words.

'I thought the poems were so good and, well , then I made a few copies of them, and then Herr Becker got a copy.'

Martin stared at her, looking so serious and furious, that she felt as if she was sitting right beside a ticking time-bomb, which was going to explode at any moment.

'And who's got the other copies?' He asked in an almost threatening tone.

'Herr Mertens, Herr Jürgens and Herr Krom - as a souvenir, I thought.'

Now Martin completely lost control.

'Are you totally mad or what? I don't believe it! Do you want to make me look ridiculous in front of everyone,' he shouted.

'I didn't mean any harm . . . I thought . . .'

'You thought! That's the worst, distributing my poems to people behind my back! Do you want to do me in? You'll not succeed! I'll never confide in you ever again! How could you be so mean and malicious and stupid! Get out of my sight! And never come back here again! I'm not going to let you make an idiot out of me! Get lost!'

Rebekka felt totally confused. She'd never seen Martin as furious as this before. It was true, he could get fairly upset at times, for instance when he didn't get any letters all week. Contact by letters was terribly important to him. Then he'd grumble out loud to himself, but he'd soon get over it, and wouldn't waste his breath on it. But he'd never lost his head like this before.

'Get lost, didn't you hear me?' He shouted at her again.

Rebekka sat there as if she was paralysed.

'Here!' He shouted and hurled his new panpipes at her feet.

'You can take these with you! I don't want anything from someone like you!'

When the panpipes hit the floor, they broke in two. Rebekka stared at the shattered instrument and then ran out of the room. She saw that Martin himself looked shocked at the extent to which he'd lost his head.

Back at home, Rebekka sat down on her sofa and began to sob uncontrollably. She was disappointed, angry and afraid at Martin's reaction. She'd never have believed that he could get as mad as that. She'd really not intended to do anything wrong. Admittedly, the secret way she'd gone about printing out and distributing the poems hadn't been right. But Martin would never have agreed to it if she'd asked him, she knew that. His reaction today was clear proof of that. She'd just wanted the teachers to read Martin's poems. Perhaps one of them would come to believe in God through reading them . . . It was always possible. Why on earth had Martin lost his head like that? She could hardly believe that he was the same nice, usually cheerful and relaxed Martin she knew.

'Martin's a total idiot! He'll see how he'll get on, without me! He can get lost, the stupid guy,' she sobbed. She sat huddled on the sofa like that for about half an hour.

Suddenly the doorbell rang. Rebekka jumped. She brushed the last tears from her cheeks and got up to answer the door. As usual, there was no one at home apart from her. Daniel was over at his girlfriend's, Dad was at his work, and Mum was at an exhibition with her friends. They had such a great family life! Martin was standing outside the door. His face was swollen from crying too, and he held out a box of chocolates, and a letter, which for once hadn't been typed on his computer.

'That's for you . . . I've been really stupid'

He didn't get any further. Rebekka took the chocolates and said, 'Come in, you . . . nutcase!' Just five minutes earlier, she'd sworn she would never speak a word to this rotten guy ever again.

The two of them sat down on the sofa, both obviously full of remorse. Eventually, Rebekka opened the box of chocolates and offered them to Martin.

'Here, do you want one?'

Martin took a chocolate. 'Thanks,' he said softly. 'Please forgive me for the way I behaved. I was just so mad. You should have asked me.'

'I know, but you'd never have let me do it, would you?' Rebekka asked.

'Probably not . . . what must the teachers think about me now? They probably think I've a screw loose!'

'Rubbish, you heard Herr Becker say they were good. And Herr Krom told me recently that the poems had made a real impression on him.'

'Honestly?'

Rebekka nodded.

'Bekki ... Can you forgive me for being such an idiot?'

Rebekka was silent, then she said, 'Martin, can you forgive me for handing out your poems behind your back?'

They smiled at each other and shook hands, without saying a word.

'You know what?' Rebekka said hesitantly. 'I'm glad you're not an angel but just an ordinary person with normal faults.'

'I wish I didn't have these faults. But perhaps it's a good thing, otherwise I'd be even more big-headed than I already am.'

'Rubbish - you're not big-headed, only a bit crazy now and then.' Rebekka laughed.

'I think I'll be able to stick the panpipes together again with super glue, and then I'll play something for you on them.'

'You'd better practice in case you have to play along with the angels in heaven,' Rebekka joked.

'Even there I won't be an angel, and I don't play the panpipes well enough for heaven, but for down here, it's okay.'

HOW MUCH LONGER?

Martin had been on the waiting list for more than a year now. His health was deteriorating. It had now got to the stage where he'd be gasping for breath, just after walking from one room to another, or if he picked up something from the floor. When the Baumanns had first moved into the house, Martin's room had been upstairs where the rest of the family's bedrooms were. It was now four months since he'd swapped his bedroom for Sven's study on the ground floor, because the stairs had become an almost insurmountable obstacle for him. He hadn't managed to walk up them for more than three months.

Rebekka often wondered how much longer it would be before the longed-for phone call about the transplant operation actually came. She was scared that Martin was not going to make it. What was it that the doctors had told him? A third of the people on the waiting list died before receiving the vital organs because there were so few available. What if Martin was part of that third?

He was amazingly laid back about it all and as cheerful as ever. If anyone asked if he was afraid that he wouldn't make it, he'd say, 'If I don't survive, then I'll be with

God. Nothing better could happen to me than to experience that. But I've got a feeling somehow, that he still wants me to stay down here. But whatever happens, God will do what is right, I'm sure of that!'

Recently, Martin had taken up a new hobby - he sketched portraits by copying photographs. They were only done in pencil but Rebekka liked his drawings.

'Look at this, Bekki. That was me when I was three.'

Rebekka looked at the sketch.

'You were really cute! Have you drawn any more over the last few days?'

Martin nodded. He showed her two more pictures.

'Who's that?' Rebekka asked.

'It's just some children. I copied them from an old magazine. You know, I'm beginning to run out of subjects to draw.'

'Do you think you could do a portrait of me?' Rebekka asked.

'Of course, if you give me a suitable photo of yourself!'

'Wait, I'll go home and get one for you. I'll be back in a couple of minutes.' She rushed away. She knew she'd be able to dig out a photo of herself from somewhere. Where would be the best place to look for some? Other people usually had an album, but it wasn't worth Rebekka's family having one because they rarely took photos. She wasn't very keen on having her's taken anyway - she always thought she looked really fat in photographs.

Mum did have a large box somewhere where all kinds of family photos were stored, the only trouble was, where? Rebekka rummaged through every drawer and cupboard in the sitting room. Finally, in the very last cupboard (that was typical!), she found a shoe-box with about a hundred photos in it. She sat down on the couch and looked through them.

Mum and Dad were in one photo, arm in arm. A rare sight! Rebekka couldn't remember ever seeing them hug each other during the course of a day. Sometimes she strongly suspected that they only acted as a married couple when they were invited to special occasions or when the whole family was staying at Aunt Marta's. Otherwise they would have had to listen to her harping on about ten golden rules for a successful marriage. She presumed that Aunt Marta's own marriage only continued to survive, because the whole family, including Uncle Arthur, had to dance to her tune.

Once again, Rebekka found herself wishing that she had a family like the Baumanns. When Herr Baumann came home from work, he gave his wife a kiss and a hug. Then he was right there for his two sons, ready to deal with any problems they might have. Rebekka had never once heard him say, 'Leave me in peace. I don't have time right now!' She heard phrases like that from her Dad all too frequently.

She came across a couple of photos taken on her last birthday. She'd invited several people along from the YPM Her Mum had arranged a buffet and it had been really great. Strangely enough, she hadn't missed the dancing and drinking that she usually experienced at parties. Maja, Markus and Gerda, (the girl who'd helped her to find the right place in the Bible, the first time she'd been along) had composed a funny song especially for her. Frank had even composed a little song too. When she really thought about it, that birthday party had been far more enjoyable than all the others put together, even though Ina didn't want to come after she'd found out it wouldn't turn into "a cool party with lots of beer."

Rebekka kept on searching. There must be a half-decent photo somewhere! By now, she'd found her childhood photos. Among them, she discovered a photo of herself, aged about four. It was really sweet and large enough for Martin to be able to make a sketch. It wasn't exactly what she'd hoped to find, but it was better than nothing. She returned the rest of the photos to the box, and put it back where she'd found it, before returning to the Baumanns' house.

'Here, do you think you'll be able to cope with this?' She asked Martin, and showed him the photo.

'I'll have a go - I'll see how it turns out.'

'Em, Martin, are you really sure that you're actually on the waiting list? I mean, you've been waiting for such a long time now, and nothing seems to be happening. Sometimes, I'm scared that they've maybe overlooked you or something.'

'I don't think so. Otherwise they wouldn't have given me a pager. I'm sure there are people who are a lot worse off than me, and who might be confined to bed. They should definitely get their turn before me. Don't worry, I'll get there - if it's meant to be.'

And what if it wasn't meant to be? Rebekka didn't like to think about it. Martin didn't look too good these days. His fingernails were dark purple and his lips were mostly that colour too, even when he'd done nothing strenuous. She really felt sorry for him (or as Gran would put it, her heart went out to him) when he gasped for breath after the slightest effort.

He didn't seem to notice it himself. When she'd once said, 'You're really wheezing badly today!' He'd looked at her in astonishment, and said, 'I'm not wheezing at all!' For him it had become a normal state of affairs.

'I'd better go home now. See you! I'll maybe come round tomorrow,' Rebekka excused herself eventually.

'Yes, see you. I'll try to finish your picture today. I can't promise you anything though.'

'Well, there's no hurry! Bye!' And she disappeared.

What did she have to do in the way of homework? Oh yes, English. They had to write an essay on the topic - "What Would Be Your Greatest Wish?" What would she write about? And it had to be in English too! If she was being honest, what she wished for the most was a boyfriend who looked exactly like Herr Becker and who was equally as nice. But of course she couldn't write that. It suddenly occurred to her what she really did wish for. She wrote, 'Most of all I wish that my friend who has got heart disease gets well soon!'

JUST WHEN YOU LEAST EXPECT IT . . .

Rebekka's phone rang. She now had her own because, according to Daniel, she'd been hogging the family's phone so much that other people couldn't make or receive calls. That wasn't true of course - the couple of hours that she used it each day weren't worth mentioning! Rebekka lay still half asleep in bed. She'd just been dreaming that Herr Deetz had asked her to write all the minor chords up on the blackboard. 'Phew! It's break time,' she shouted out loud.

It was only when the telephone rang again for the second time that she woke up with a start. She peered at her radio-alarm. It was ten minutes past six. What idiot was calling her as early as this on a Saturday morning when they didn't even have school! She'd give them a piece of her mind, for depriving her of sleep like that!

'Rebekka Jansen here,' she snarled into the handset.

'Hello, Bekki. It's Sven here.'

'Sven?' What in the world was he phoning her for at this time of the morning?

'I just wanted to let you know, that the university clinic phoned at midnight, and Martin was called in for the transplant operation. Mum went with him.'

Suddenly Rebekka was wide awake.

'What? Martin's gone off for the operation? And what's happened?'

'Unfortunately, I can't tell you much more. Mum phoned half an hour ago and said that they'd just taken Martin into the operating theatre. They're probably operating on him at this very moment.' Sven sounded both excited and afraid.

Rebekka felt quite queasy too.

'Was Martin . . . very nervous?' She asked after a while.

'It was all okay. Actually, he was fairly laid back. You know what he's like. He trusts totally in God, and that gives him an extraordinary calmness. Mum even told me that he'd acted out some sketches for her, to cheer her up, while they were waiting for the anaesthetist.'

'He's crazy! Man, I'd never have dreamed it would happen today! Please phone me right away, if you hear any more news.'

'I'll do that, Bekki. Well, I'll have to let some other people know about it too. I'll phone later. See you. Bye.'

'Okay, and thanks a lot for phoning!'

Rebekka put down the receiver and sat for a while, trying to grasp what she'd just heard Sven telling her. It had happened at last! Now, when she'd least expected it. How was Martin getting on right now? How long would the operation go on for?

Suddenly, Rebekka felt that she really needed to talk

to someone. But who? Mum? Dad was away on a business trip and they couldn't contact him. She walked quietly along to the bedroom and tapped on the door.

'Mum,' she called softly, 'It's Bekki. I have to talk to you.'

'Come in, if you really have to,' came the not exactly welcoming response. Mum had been asleep. It surprised Rebekka that even though her mother was a light sleeper, she'd only been wakened by her knocking and not by the phone ringing.

'What's wrong?' Frau Jansen asked, irritably.

'They took Martin in for his transplant operation last night,' Rebekka explained and struggled not to burst into tears.

'What? Your friend who's been on the waiting list for so long?' Apparently, Mum had occasionally taken in some information when Rebekka had attempted to tell her about Martin.

Rebekka nodded, 'He's being operated on right now. I'm so scared . . . If he dies now . . .'

'Oh dear, Bekki, my girl!' Frau Jansen said, and gave her a hug. When was the last time she'd done that? Rebekka couldn't remember.

'Your Martin will get through it. We'll keep our fingers crossed for him, won't we?'

'That's no use and you know it. In a situation like this, Martin would say, "Come on, Bekki, let's pray about it!"'

'You believe in God too now, Bekki, don't you?'

Rebekka nodded.

'You know, sometimes I wish I could still believe too. It all seems so long ago now. When I was little, your

Gran used to pray with me, and I believed in God. But then Ewald came along,' (that was Dad), 'and we had to work hard on the house, and there was so much to do . . . and most of Ewald's friends weren't believers. It must have been around that time that I stopped . . . but you've got other things on your mind right now.'

Frau Jansen had never spoken like that with her daughter before.

'Please, carry on, Mum,' Rebekka begged.

'Oh,' Frau Jansen protested, 'It's too late now anyway.'

Rebekka looked at her, 'It's not too late! At the YPM we heard a story about a boy who ran away from home and frittered away all of the money he'd inherited. And then when everything went completely wrong for him, he went back to his father who gladly accepted him back. Markus said that God is like that father, and that you can always come back to him.'

'I vaguely remember that story. Gran often told it to me. But I feel guilty before God. I haven't bothered about him for so long. He's so far away, but I do envy people who can trust in him, the way I used to myself.'

'Then just come back to him!'

'I can't, Bekki. Not yet . . . I wouldn't know what to say to God.'

'Can I pray with you, Mum?'

Frau Jansen said nothing and looked down at the floor. Then she nodded. Rebekka closed her eyes and clasped her hands.

'Father, you've heard what Mum has just said. You see that she wants to come back to you and is a bit wary about it. Yet, you still love her! You'll please let her know that, won't you? I think it would be fantastic, if Mum belonged to you again! Thank you for promising not to turn away anyone who comes to you. Father, you know as well, what they're doing with Martin right now. I'm scared. Help me to trust in you like Martin always does. You'll get him through the transplant operation, won't you? Martin said that you'll do the right thing. Thank you that you're with him . . . then nothing can actually go wrong. Be very close to us! Amen.'

Rebekka looked across at her mother.

'Thank you, Bekki,' she said quietly. 'I don't know - perhaps I really should trust in God again. But I still need time. But in spite of that - thanks. How do you know that they took Martin in last night?'

'Sven phoned me. He'll call back when he has any more news . Oh, Mum, I really hope it goes well! If only I could do something, even if it was only something small! Apart from praying, I mean.'

'You can't do anything for Martin now. You'll just have to wait.'

It was a strange feeling, sitting beside Mum and talking with her as if it was the most natural thing in the world. Over the last few years she and Rebekka had usually had nothing much to say to one another apart from 'Have you seen the car keys?' Or 'Have you finished your homework?' And only things like that. Rebekka had always had the feeling that her mother didn't like her very much and that she saw her only as an annoying hanger-on.

And now they were sitting together, and could talk to each other, and Mum was listening to her - she was really listening to her at last, without thinking about rushing off to the arts centre or somewhere else. It was great!

Rebekka had a long conversation with her mother. It was a woman to woman talk, or rather a daughter to mother and a mother to daughter talk. Rebekka told her about everything she'd gone through recently with Martin, about the people at the YPM, about the private tuition and lots of other stuff. And Mum listened to it all.

When Rebekka paused for breath, after her torrent of words, her Mum said, 'I think I haven't given you enough attention. You're my daughter and I hardly know you. Bekki, that will have to change. Please talk to me about everything you want to in future. And tell me off if I don't spend time with you!'

Suddenly the phone rang. Rebekka galloped over to answer it.

'Jansen,' she answered it, nervously.

'Hello, Bekki pet. It's Gran here. You sound a bit excited.'

'Hello, Gran. Yes, Martin went away to have his transplant operation last night and I thought it was Sven phoning. That's his brother - he's going to tell me how everything's gone, as soon as he knows.'

'What? Martin is being operated on today? I'll pray for him that it'll go well, little Bekki.'

'Yes, Gran. Please do that. Did you phone for any particular reason? Because I'd prefer to hang up in case Sven is trying to phone us!'

'But he'll surely ring you on your own phone. Let me have a word with your Mum.'

Gran was right. Sven would definitely not ring up the family's telephone number, so Rebekka passed the receiver to her Mum and returned to her room.

She could hardly bear the suspense. It was worse because she was on her own and had nothing to distract her from what was happening. She wondered how Sven could stand it either. Perhaps he'd already heard something fresh and had forgotten to call her. It was now 10 o'clock. There must be news by now!

She ran to her phone and dialled the Baumanns' number. It was engaged. Bother! She sat down again on the sofa. What could she do now? She leafed through her old *Asterix* comics and tried to take her mind off things. But it was no use, she kept thinking about Martin. So she put the comics away again. Instead, she took Martin's poems out of her writing desk drawer. She still had the original print-outs. She skimmed through the pages until one poem caught her attention. It was called 'Living with Death.' She read it.

Help me to realise that I could die at any time,
and that I won't live for ever on this earth!
Help me to realise that after death
I'll stand before you.

How often I make plans about my future life,
and I think that time will never end,
But if I died tonight,
All the plans would be in vain,
Do I really make the most of today?

What do I have to put right,
What do I still have to do?
Where do you need me, here and now?
I want to live in such a way,

that I could easily come to you
today, if it's meant to be.

Therefore I'll behave like that today,
and use my time,
and live in such a way that you can use me!
I leave my time in your hands and I'm ready,
to die, at the time you have planned for me.

Rebekka read through the poem twice. She realised that Martin wasn't really concerned about living a long life, but instead he wanted to use his time for God, no matter how long or short it was. And he was also ready to die, if God wanted that.

In some ways, Rebekka felt comforted by the poem, but in other ways, she could not be indifferent to whether Martin died or not. He was her best friend and she wanted him to live! She sat for ages, engrossed in her thoughts and failing to notice how much time had gone by. Her mother had gone over to her Gran's ages ago. Gran had urgently needed to see her. Out of habit, she'd forgotten to say goodbye to Rebekka.

It was only when her phone rang that Rebekka jumped.

'Rebekka Jansen here!' She yelled into it.

'Hi, Bekki, it's Sven here again.'

Rebekka held her breath.

'Mum's just phoned. Martin's had his operation and has come through everything very well so far, the doctors say. Of course, he's still unconscious and they're keeping him breathing artificially, but otherwise everything has gone really well. Mum's going to stay there and keep us up to date with what's happening by phone.' Sven's voice sounded relieved and relaxed, and Rebekka felt as if a huge weight had been removed from her too.

'Thanks for calling. You can't imagine how happy I am to hear that!'

'Yes, I can,' Sven said, 'By the way, I was supposed to give you something that Martin left behind for you before he and Mum took off last night. You can pick it up from here any time you want. I suppose you'll be coming round here soon?'

'Of course!' Rebekka promised.

What could Sven have for her over there?

A NEW BEGINNING

Rebekka couldn't wait at home any longer. She was had to see what Martin had given her. Sven hadn't wanted to give away the secret. He'd only said it was something personal. What could it be? Rebekka quickly got dressed - she had still been wearing her pyjamas - and set off. Sven answered the door.

'Hello, Bekki. I thought you'd call round soon.'

They sat down in the sitting room.

'Has your mother phoned again?' Rebekka asked.

Sven shook his head. 'No. She's probably not allowed to see Martin yet. He's in the intensive care unit, where he's being observed around the clock. We certainly won't find out anything new before tomorrow.'

Well, the main thing was that Martin had survived the operation.

'By the way, what did you get for me from Martin?' Rebekka couldn't bear the suspense any longer.

'Oh yes! Wait a moment, I'll fetch it for you.'

Sven left the room and returned a moment later, holding a picture. He handed it to Rebekka, 'Here, he drew that last night. Is it you?'

She nodded.

'Hey, you were quite cute in a strange sort of way!' Sven said.

Did he think that she could never have been cute? She looked at the drawing. It was lovely.

'Perhaps this is my last keepsake from Martin,' the thought went through her head. No, Martin had got through his operation, what could happen now?

'How did it all happen last night? Did Martin's pager go off suddenly?' Rebekka asked after a while.

'No, the phone rang at five minutes past midnight. Martin wasn't asleep, but because he thought it might just be a drunk or someone like that phoning, he didn't answer the phone at first. That kind of thing sometimes happens. But then the ringing annoyed him so much that he answered it. It was actually the surgeon who was going to operate on Martin, and he asked him to go to the university hospital as soon as possible.'

'Martin must have had a huge shock!'

'No, he didn't seem to take it like that. He woke my mother and me up. Mum thought at first that Martin had just been dreaming. To be on the safe side, she phoned up the hospital, and they confirmed the message Martin had received. Then I phoned for a taxi - Mum was far too uptight to drive. Dad's away on a business trip in Spain at the moment. Who would have thought that it would happen now of all times! But Mum called him from the hospital and he's going to try and catch the next flight back.'

'Have you had your lunch?' Rebekka asked, as her stomach had begun to rumble loudly. It was almost the afternoon now, after all.

'No, in the excitement, I completely forgot about it. But we've got a pizza in the freezer. It's far too big for me to eat by myself. Do you want to share it with me?'

'Good idea!' Pizza was just the right thing to have.

While they tucked in, Sven told her about various tricks he'd played on people in the past. It was really funny to listen to, and more importantly, it took Rebekka's mind off thinking about Martin all the time.

At about four o'clock the phone rang. Sven picked it up and said 'Sven Baumann here...' Rebekka listened in as Sven continued to speak to the caller on the other end. 'How's it going? . . . Uh-huh . . . em . . . Yes, I have. She's here. We've just eaten some pizza . . . And when can you visit him? Tomorrow . . . Yes, of course, I'll come too . . . Bekki as well? . . . Oh, I see! . . . Right, I'll do that . . . I've done that . . . Yes, you too! Go and have a good sleep, you'll need it! . . . Okay, I'll tell him . . . Bye!'

He put the receiver down.

'Was that your mother?' Rebekka asked.

'Yes, she's phoned the intensive care unit again. Everything's super. No problems. Mum's going to stay there. She's found a room where she can stay for up to a week. If everything continues to go well, she thinks that we can visit Martin briefly tomorrow. We should go round to the hospital tomorrow in any case, that is, if you want to!'

What a silly question! She wanted to see Martin again at last. She wondered if he looked any different now. How was he feeling with the new organs in his body? It must be a weird feeling.

'I'd better phone everyone and tell them how Martin's

getting on. You know, there are a lot of people from church who are praying for him and waiting for news. I'll have to tell our relatives too and there are quite a lot of them. Then I'll have to go to the hospital and take Mum some clothes and stuff. She wasn't prepared for a stay there.'

Rebekka understood. She couldn't help much by staying there. But it had been good to spend the last few hours with Sven, and at least she now knew that Martin was getting on okay under the circumstances.

First thing the next morning she went to her Gran's. For the past few months she'd got into the habit of going to church with her most Sundays.

'How's your friend Martin?' Gran wanted to know immediately. 'I was praying constantly for him yesterday. He's got through it, I hope?'

Rebekka nodded. 'So far, he's okay. If there are no complications, I'm hoping to see him this afternoon.'

Gran looked at her in astonishment, 'As soon as this? I thought that after such a big operation he'd have to be kept behind glass for weeks and not be allowed any visitors. You must have misunderstood what they said to you. I really can't imagine that they'd let the poor boy have visitors today.'

Rebekka left it at that. There was little point in arguing with Gran's opinions, she knew. She didn't get much out of the sermon, she kept thinking about Martin and how he was getting on. Had he come round after the anaesthetic yet? Hopefully the visit would go ahead in the afternoon!

The news of Martin's transplant operation had spread like wildfire - in a country village like this everyone knew each other and Gran had no doubt contributed. So, after the church service, Rebekka was surrounded by lots of people who wanted to know how Martin was. Everyone knew that they were good friends.

'We're thinking about Martin. We're praying for him.'

'I really hope he gets better soon.'

'Oh yes, he really deserves everything to go well for him!'

They all really seemed to care about Martin, and she was a bit taken aback at it all. Usually, people didn't seem to bother about him, or had she just not noticed?

At lunch-time she phoned the Baumanns.

'Herr Baumann here,' Martin's father answered in his deep, warm sounding voice. So he was at home again.

'Hello, Simon. It's Bekki here. I wanted to ask if you're going to visit Martin this afternoon, and if so, can I come too?' Rebekka had been on first name terms with Martin's parents for a couple of months now, which made her feel that she belonged.

'Yes, we're going there in any case. You can certainly come along. But I can't promise that they'll let us actually see Martin. Karin phoned earlier and told us that he is slowly coming round. But naturally, he's still very weak, and attached to a lot of tubes and things.'

'What time are you setting off?' Rebekka asked.

'At about three. We can come and pick you up at your house.'

'Okay, I'll be ready. And thanks again. Bye.'

'Not at all! Bye, Bekki.'

At last it was 3 o'clock. Rebekka waited impatiently at her front door, when she heard the Baumanns' Golf pulling up. They needn't have bothered to toot the horn, because she came shooting out like a rocket.

'Let's go!' She said, after slamming the car door shut. It was so irritating that they had to stick to the speed limit in the area. At least, it really annoyed Rebekka today. But even the longest car journey eventually comes to an end, and at about quarter past four, they arrived at the university hospital. Karin Baumann was waiting for them. Together they walked to the intensive care unit. Rebekka felt a bit queasy when she saw many people attached to lots of tubes, being wheeled along the long corridors.

She hoped she'd never end up here herself.

When they reached the intensive care unit, a nurse met them.

'You can't come in as you are. You'll have to change first. Who do you want to go and see?'

'We want to know how Martin Baumann is getting on, and if we can visit him now.'

'Just a moment, please. I'll have to ask the doctor first.' She hurried away and returned about five minutes later, which felt like an eternity to Rebekka.

'One or two people may see him, in whatever order you'd like to go in. But it can only be for a very short time, please!'

The four of them decided that Frau Baumann should go to see him first. Before they allowed her in, she had to put on a green gown, gloves and a mask, and cover her hair with a sort of cap, and put on disinfected rubber shoes. She could easily have been mistaken for a surgeon ready to begin an operation.

She stayed for only about three minutes with Martin, and she then beckoned Rebekka to go in.

'Bekki, get changed. Martin wants to see you!'

Rebekka changed at high speed. 'He'll never recognise me like this!' She thought, when she looked at herself. But there was nothing for it, she had to wear the stuff. Cautiously, she entered the room. There were machines everywhere. It was really creepy. Then she spotted Martin and was shocked. He was connected to numerous tubes and when she first saw him he looked the worse for wear. But when she went nearer, it struck her that Martin didn't have blue lips and fingernails any more. It looked like he'd put on some lipstick, because his lips were a normal red colour now and his hands looked healthy and pink.

'Martin,' Rebekka whispered, 'It's me, Bekki!'

'Bekki,' Martin whispered back in an even quieter voice, 'Did you . . . get the picture?'

Rebekka nodded. 'I showed it to my Mother. She said you were a good artist . . . Lots of people from church and my Gran send you their best wishes. She's praying for you too . . . I'm so happy that you've got through it all. At least, the first part of it.'

'You're great, Bekki,' Martin said in a weak voice.

'You are, too, Martin,' Rebekka just managed to say before the nurse shoved her out of the room again.

'He needs rest now,' she explained.

'Why has he got such a hoarse voice?' Rebekka asked.

'We only removed a breathing tube about three-quarters of an hour ago, and that's affected the vocal cords a bit, but they'll soon be back to normal again.'

After Rebekka had changed again, she, Sven, and Herr Baumann went home again. Frau Baumann preferred to stay in her room at the hospital, so that she'd be near Martin, in case anything unexpected happened. Sven and Herr Baumann weren't allowed to visit Martin because he would have found it too exhausting, but they hoped to see him the next day.

When Rebekka was back in her room, she sat down on her bed and thought about the afternoon. It was brilliant, that everything had gone so smoothly with the organs transplant. Eventually, Rebekka clasped her hands and prayed, 'Father, thank you that Martin's got through it. Now everything's going to be alright. It'll be a new beginning. Thank you! You are really brilliant. It's good that you're watching over Martin's new life. I'm excited about what you've got planned for him and for us in the future.'

EPILOGUE
from the author
Heidi Schmidt

Martin's Last Chance is a little like an autobiography. I've experienced similar or identical events to Martin's in my own life. Although several of the characters are completely fictitious, the character of Rebekka represents several people who have played a role in my life to a greater or lesser extent. Other people who I have portrayed in the story actually exist. The private tuition, sketches, pager, wheelchair and birthday party are also all taken from my own experiences.

Many people may think that it all sounds too simple, and that it must have been more dramatic than that. Perhaps some may think that I (Martin) must have gone through an inner struggle and have been afraid before making the decision whether or not to have the transplant operation. But that wasn't the case. Thanks to my experience of God, I knew for sure that He would let only what was best for me happen.

You always have to be prepared for surprises, as far as God is concerned, I felt that the transplant operation was simply one of God's great ideas, and I was convinced that He knew what He was doing. I was curious to discover what would happen next. I know that this attitude was a gift from God, and that most people waiting for a transplant operation don't go through that time in such a relaxed and happy way. Therefore, I can completely understand if some people think that this story is not credible. However, the fact remains that that's the way it was with me.

It's five years since I had my heart and lungs transplant operation. On the whole, I'm really well nowadays. Naturally, I'll be under medical supervision for the rest of my life, and I have to take medication.

So, what happened to me after the operation? Well, I passed my school leaving exams, thanks to my private tutors. I then got married, and my husband and I attended Bible College. After a year and a half I gave up the training as a deaconess. It seemed to make more sense, for me to do practical work in our church. My husband finished training and he now works as a Deacon I help out in our church and in three other churches, and I help to take children's meetings, lead Bible Studies, Youth Fellowships, Young People's Meetings, and give RE lessons in nursery school, and help with sermons etc. Telling people about God's love makes me very happy.

The story about Rebekka and Martin doesn't just describe how a person coped while waiting for a transplant operation, but it shows above all that it is worthwhile living under God's guidance.

Over and over again I have discovered that you can

totally rely on God, no matter how difficult the situation is. He wants the best for us because He loves us like a good Father.

I hope that everyone who reads this story will come to know God as their loving Father, as I have.

Heidi Schmidt
1996

If you would like to write to Heidi Schmidt, please contact her, care of Christian Focus Publications at the address in the front of the book or you can write to her directly at

Heidi Schmidt
Lindenstr. 19
38471 Brechtorf
Deutschland

The Freedom Fighter
William Wilberforce
by Derick Bingham

'No! No!' cried the little boy, 'I want to stay with my mother!' A man pulled his mother from him and offered for sale, immediately. They were to be separated for the rest of their lives. This was the fate of thousands of people in the days before slavery was abolished. One man fought to end the terrors of the slave trade. His name was William Wilberforce. His exciting story shows the amazing effect his faith in Christ and his love for people had on transforming a nation.

'A story deserving to be told to a new generation.'
The Prime Minister the Rt. Hon. Tony Blair, M.P.

ISBN 1-85792-371-5

The Watchmaker's Daughter
Corrie Ten Boom
by Jean Watson

Corrie loved to help others, especially handicapped children. But her happy lifestyle in Holland is shattered when she is sent to a Nazi concentration camp. She suffered hardship and punishment but experienced God's love and help in unbearable situations. This is a story of adventure, courage and faith. Discover about one of the most outstanding Christian women of the 20th century.

ISBN 1-85792-116-X

A Voice In The Dark
Richard Wurmbrand
by Catherine Mackenzie

'Where am I? Where are you taking me?' Richard's voice cracked under the strain. Gasping for air he realized - this was the nightmare! When Richard Wurmbrand is arrested, imprisoned and tortured, he finds himself in utter darkness. Yet the people who put him there discover that their prisoner has a light which can still be seen in the dark - the love of God. This story of faith, despite horrific persecution, is unforgettable and will be an inspiration to all who read it.

ISBN 1-85792-298-0

From Wales to Westminster
Martyn Lloyd-Jones
by his grand-son
Christopher Catherwood

'Fire! Fire! - A woman shouted frantically. But the Lloyd-Jones family slept, blissfully ignorant that their family home was just about to go up in smoke. Martyn, aged ten, was snug in his bed, but his life was in danger. What happened to Martyn? Who rescued him? How did the fire affect him and his family? And why is somebody writing a book about Martyn in the first place? In this book Christopher Catherwood, Martyn's grandson, tells you about the amazing life of his grandfather, Dr. Martyn Lloyd Jones. Find out about the young boy who trained to be a doctor at just sixteen years old. Meet the young man who was destined to become the Queen's surgeon and find out why he gave it all up to work for God.

ISBN 1-85792-349-9

LOOK OUT

FOR THE

FOLLOWING

NEW

Hudson Taylor
~ An Adventure Begins ~
by Catherine Mackenzie

GEORGE MULLER
~ The children's champion ~
by Irene Howat

Look out for our

New Fiction Titles

Something to Shout About - Sheila Jacobs.
Jane is back in her old home town of Gipley but things aren't what she'd expected. Heather's mum has a slimey new boyfriend and Heron has a really good looking brother called Woody. Woody agrees to help the girls spear head a 'Save our Church' campaign - soon everyone is up to their necks in slogans, banners and campaign strategies. But has anyone thought about asking God what he thinks? Jane learns a valuable lesson about prayer and finding out about what God's will is.

Twice Freed - Patricia St. John.
Onesimus is a slave in Philemon's household. All he has ever wanted is to live his life in freedom. He wants nothing to do with Jesus Christ or, the man, Paul, who preaches about him. One day Onesimus steals some money from his master. Find out what happens and if Onesimus realises the meaning of true freedom!

CHRISTIAN FOCUS

Good books with the real message of hope!

Christian Focus Publications publishes biblically-accurate books for adults and children.

If you are looking for quality bible teaching for children then we have a wide and excellent range of bible story books - from board books to teenage fiction, we have it covered.

You can also try our new Bible teaching Syllabus for 3-9 year olds and teaching materials for pre-school children.

These children's books are bright, fun and full of biblical truth, an ideal way to help children discover Jesus Christ for themselves. Our aim is to help children find out about God and get them enthusiastic about reading the Bible, now and later in their life.

**Find us at our web page:
www.christianfocus.com**